Defending Jessica

By

Benna Bos

©2022 by Benna Bos
Flashpoint Publications
First edition November, 2022

ISBN 978-1-61929-486-8

Cover Design by AcornGraphics

Editors Verda Foster and Staci Blevins

Publisher's Note:

Acknowledgments

I fell in love with Agnes and Helen when I wrote the first book in this series, but it might never have happened without the people who encouraged my love of writing, my desire to express myself, and the people and places that inspire me. So, Amy, Rhonna, and Valerie: thank you for reading every word I wrote and telling me you loved it. Kelly and Patty: thank you for taking a chance on me. San Francisco: I love you, my city. Don't let anybody talk shit about you. Finally, to my two partners in life for supporting me in everything I do, my spouse and my dog: Love you both!

Dedication

For Katrina

Chapter One

Worst client ever.

It was all Veronica Turner could think as she walked out of the county jail. An hour in Jessica French's presence was equivalent to days of psychological torture. She slammed her hip into the metal bar on the exit door and considered calling her cousin Malcolm to officially disown him for getting her into this.

Sharp clicks echoed her frustration as her heels hit the concrete steps. By the time she reached the sidewalk, she stopped, took a deep breath, and made up her mind. As her ears filled with the sounds of nearby I-80, she smiled to herself and tucked her thick, blonde hair behind her ear. No challenge was too big for Veronica Turner. She would not back down from defending the most unlikable client in the history of forever.

She needed an angle. It wasn't so much about a defense at this early stage as a change in the tide. It was too easy to believe that someone as deeply flawed as Jessica French was a killer. If Veronica allowed her client to get swept up in the wave of dislike, every newscaster in the country would be calling for her blood. By the time they reached the trial, Jessica would be all but convicted before the jury was even chosen.

Veronica didn't build her reputation on riding tides; she made it on changing them. If she was going to defend this woman from murder charges, she needed to control everything she could, including public perception. And that thought led to a great idea.

She picked up her pace, practically running—or as close to running as she would ever get on her thin, but short legs—to her car. Veronica slipped inside the quiet, leather-covered interior, her suit skirt hiking up. She ignored that but pulled the silk blouse out of the waistband because no matter how thin her mother claimed she was, she needed breathing room. She fished her phone out of her designer purse and held it up, staring at her face for a moment, her blue eyes reflecting back to her from the dark glass.

It only took a moment for Veronica to make up her mind. That's how she'd always been. Snap decision, that's what her father called it. He said it was a gift. Her mother thought it was a curse. But Veronica knew her instincts had helped her clients many times over. On that gritty San Francisco sidewalk in front of the jail moments ago, Veronica made a decision that just might save Jessica French's life. And she intended to act on it.

"Veronica?"

Something about caller ID pissed her off. She missed being able to tell the person on the other line who she was. Maybe it was a sense of entrance. Veronica liked to make an entrance.

"Hi, Agnes. Do you have a minute?"

"For you, always."

Veronica smirked. Having people owe her created collateral she was always willing to take advantage of. That she had represented Agnes's wife when she was accused of murder was about to pay off. "I need a favor."

"Anything. You know that."

"I'm representing Jessica French."

"I heard. Did you go see her yet? Is she as awful as they say?"

Veronica let out a breath. "Worse."

"Damn. I'm sorry. I heard Malcolm talked you into it. He trained her dog, right?"

Veronica rolled her eyes. Even though Agnes couldn't see it, she was pretty sure the sentiment came across in her voice. "Yeah. And I heard he talked your wife into keeping the dog."

"Wait. What?"

Veronica couldn't stop the chuckle that escaped. "She didn't tell you yet, eh? Well, you'll probably find out tonight because Malcolm's newest dog project is aggressing toward the poor little thing, so he can't keep her. I'm pretty sure Pookie's on her way to your house right now."

"Pookie? Really? Shit." Agnes let out a deep breath.

"Your cousin can talk my wife into anything."

"Yeah, well, he was married to her first. I guess there's something to that."

"Thanks for the reminder. I needed that." Sarcasm dripped from Agnes's tone.

As amusing as the vision of a tiny terror yipping at Agnes's heels was, and as much as Veronica enjoyed provoking her, there was business to conduct. "Look, marriage drama aside, I need help."

Agnes must have snapped back to the conversation at hand. "Yeah. Right. Okay. What can I do for you?"

Veronica knew that what always worked for her would work now. So she made sure her tone gave no room for argument, no room for discussion. It was a borderline demand. "I need you to do a podcast on Jessica."

An expected silence followed her statement. It stretched out over the phone line like a long piece of cotton batting, dampening the sound. Veronica held her breath. She needed Agnes's clout for this. Since leaving her job at the *True Crime Tonight* television show to focus on her podcast *Murder by the Bay*, Agnes had gained even more fans, surprising Veronica's cynical take on the career change. But now Agnes's bizarre choice benefited Veronica.

The problem was, Veronica knew Agnes had a list of worthy innocents waiting to have her give publicity to their case and seed doubt of their guilt to the crime junkies addicted to her show. An evil narcissist widely hated by anyone who came into contact with her would not be high on Agnes's altruistic list. And Veronica knew it.

Veronica broke into the silence like a persuasive con artist. "Malcolm talked me into taking this case because he's absolutely convinced Jessica is innocent."

White noise traveled through the phone line. Veronica tried to pull on Agnes's personal heartstrings, and do it in a way that gently reminded her of the debt she owed. "Kinda like when Helen was accused of murder. Only she didn't do it."

The sigh Agnes expelled was audible despite the physical distance between them. Sure, it was a low blow. It's not like Agnes needed to be reminded of the intense few weeks when Helen was suspected of killing her previous girlfriend, or that Veronica had helped her navigate her way through the interrogations with the police.

But Veronica's guilt trip seemed to be working when Agnes finally spoke. "Malcolm told me about it. I mean, maybe Jessica French is innocent, but she's such a—"

"Bitch," Veronica finished for her. "Yeah. She sure is. But an innocent one."

"Would she even do the podcast?"

"She'll do it. She knows I'm her best shot at getting a fair trial. She'll do what I tell her to do."

A snort echoed through the phone. "I think getting her off will be hard. Unless you can change the venue to Alaska where maybe they haven't seen her taunt reporters and insecure men on television. But it's not happening anywhere in California. Also, her pillows suck. Kimber and Jasper have eaten three between them."

Veronica rolled her eyes again. She wished like hell her already rich client hadn't gotten the urge to create a line of throw pillows so cheaply made that Helen and Agnes's mutts had no trouble ripping them to shreds. "That's where you come in, my friend. I need to get her story out there. We know there's no such thing as an impartial jury in all of this. So we need to get people on our side."

"Okay. Two things. First, I do shows on the innocent accused, yes, but not with an agenda other than to expose the truth. If I find evidence of my subject's guilt, I don't hide it."

"I know. And I wouldn't even propose this if I wasn't totally sure Jessica is completely innocent of this crime." Veronica smiled with pride. She didn't like being lectured, but she couldn't afford to give Agnes any guff at the moment. So, she'd made her tone as smooth as marble. She swallowed back her self-righteous urge to stick up for herself, knowing it wouldn't get her what she wanted. But no matter how successful she was, it still stung like hell.

"Second, I'm not sure you'll be doing her a favor. That woman has a long history of coming across terrible in the media. I don't know why you think she'd look better on the podcast."

"Leave that to me, Agnes. I'm glad you're up for the challenge. I'll call Heath to schedule the first interview. Thanks. Bye." Veronica hung up before Agnes had a chance to argue. She'd just completely railroaded her friend, which included picking Agnes's less confrontational partner to schedule their meeting. But sometimes that was the only way to get things done.

Veronica smiled to herself as she started the car. She had reluctantly taken on the biggest hurdle she'd ever had to jump in her career, but she'd figured out how to cross it. And, as always, she would prevail.

****

Kaia Kent shoved the last piece of equipment in her bag and hefted it over her shoulder. Despite her short stature, she was strong and perfectly capable of handling the heavy bag. Her short, brown hair bounced over her forehead as she turned to wave goodbye to Elsa McReedy and headed toward her pick-up.

She couldn't resist grinning to herself when her back was to the elderly woman and her kind caregiver. She'd just successfully completed her first solo project at her new job and it felt good, really good.

Agnes probably hadn't planned to let Kaia loose so soon into her employment with the *Murder by the Bay* podcast, but Agnes and her wife had some sort of appointment with the adoption agency, so she had no choice. Opportunity seized, Kaia hoped she'd nailed it.

Elsa McReedy had spilled her son's deepest secrets, leading anyone listening to the audio recording to believe that it was Ken McReedy who murdered his wife's lover, rather than poor Terry McReedy, who was currently in prison for the deed.

Kaia pushed her bags into the back of her truck and shut the door of the topper. Her old blue pick-up stuck out like a sore thumb in a city of small, practical cars. But she needed the space for her gear, and she liked the feel of the bench seat beneath her as she rode down the street. It felt like home, no matter how many thousands of miles away Ohio was now.

She wrenched open the driver's side door of her truck and jumped onto the seat. The little hop was necessary because her five-foot nothing stature didn't lend itself to the leg length she needed for a smooth entrance. But she didn't care. Short or not, she could drive her truck, and she was proud of it.

Just as she was about to crank the key in the starter, her cell phone rang. She reached into her bag and extracted the battered device; its cracked face and dirty case showed the wear and tear of its difficult life. The caller ID indicated that the call was being forwarded from her predecessor's line.

"Hello?"

"Um…I'm looking for Heath."

"Heath is no longer at this number. If you're calling about the podcast, I can help you. I'm Kaia Kent. I took over for Heath."

A deep breath echoed through the tiny holes at the top of Kaia's phone. "What happened to Heath?"

"He took another job and specifically recommended me to take over for him. How can I help you?"

The feminine tone on the other end of the line grew harsh. "What other job? He's basically Agnes's best friend. Why the hell would he leave her?"

Kaia wasn't certain how much information she should give this stranger. After all, she had no idea who this person even was. "Um. May I ask who's calling?"

"You may ask. I might not answer."

Kaia pulled the phone away from her ear and stared at it. Was this for real? She hadn't spoken to someone so rude and immature since high school.

Deeply out of her comfort zone, Kaia shifted gears and tried a different tactic. "Um. Maybe I should have Agnes call you back."

"No. I'm calling to schedule an interview. I don't want to screw around. Now where did Heath go?"

Instantly transported to her middle school when she cut

off her hair and started wearing baggy pants and boots, Kaia knew she had to stand up to bullies. And this woman, whoever she was, was a high-class, first-rate, snotty-ass bully. Kaia hardened her tone. "How can I help you?"

The caller let out a breath so hard it hit the phone like a hurricane. "I'm Veronica Turner."

Kaia had heard of Veronica Turner. She knew the powerhouse attorney was reputed to be a woman not to be messed with. Veronica was supposedly a terrifying human being full of bluff and bluster. In their short conversation, the woman had already lived up to her reputation. "Um. Okay. And?"

"And, I need to schedule an interview with my client. Agnes has already agreed to it. Didn't she tell you?"

Agnes had mentioned that they were starting a new case, but she'd completely left out the tidbit about this horrible woman. Now that she knew this wasn't some crazy ex of Heath's, but an actual story, she slouched in her seat. Had she already blown this?

"Um, yes. Of course." Kaia fumbled with her bag in a desperate attempt to extract the planner she carried with her everywhere. The kinesthetic learner crutch was one she'd never given up. "Give me just a minute."

"I think we've wasted enough time, don't you?" Veronica's harsh voice left no room for argument.

Kaia managed to grab hold of the small booklet only to have it leap from her fingers and land on the floor of the truck. She frantically unbuckled her seatbelt and leaned over to try to extract the thing.

"Hello? Are you there?"

Kaia gripped the planner between her fingers and sprang upright in the seat. "Yes. Yes. I'm here."

"My client can meet with Agnes on Monday at 11 a.m. Please schedule a two-hour meeting for that time. Be at the jail and ready to record at least ten minutes prior."

Kaia glanced at the planner. Agnes had another meeting scheduled at that time. "I'm afraid that won't work for us."

"Make it work." The harsh words were followed by the distinctive sound of a dial tone indicating the insufferable woman had hung up.

Kaia threw the phone onto the seat beside her and leaned back, running her hands over her face. Difficult people were going to come with the territory of this job, but that woman took it to a whole new level. The entire drive home Kaia's mind whirled with thoughts of Veronica Turner. By the time she'd parked in the open lot behind her building—the only place she could put the truck because it was too tall to fit in the parking garage—her phone rang again.

"Hi, Agnes."

"I heard you had the pleasure of talking to Malcolm's cousin."

Kaia had once met Helen's ex-husband, Malcolm. He was a kind, charming man, nothing like his beastly cousin. "Um, yeah. She called a few minutes ago."

"Yeah. She's a handful. Sorry about that. I'll reschedule my meeting so we can make it to the jail for the interview. Are you good to do the work on Monday?"

Obviously, Veronica held just as much sway as she thought she did. "I can be there."

"Cool. Let's ride together. See you then. Have a good weekend."

Kaia hung up the phone with the realization that she failed to ask Agnes one essential question. Was that nightmare of a woman going to be at the interview?

Chapter Two

For some reason Veronica had yet to fully understand, she was at her most relaxed when she was out with Teresa and Monica. They weren't particularly old friends; she'd known them for about a year. They were lovely people, of course, always quick with a joke or a smile. But that described a lot of people she spent time with.

As she watched the bodies twisting together on the club's dance floor, she wondered if it was the places they went. Other friends always wanted to go to bars or clubs filled with hungry, slavering men desperate to take a woman—any woman—home. That atmosphere always made her, and usually most of her companions, tense. But that wasn't the kind of places she went with Teresa and Monica.

Teresa swung her glass in Veronica's direction, her lack of small motor skills gave away how much of the golden liquid inside she'd already consumed. "So why did you break up with Ken?"

Veronica shrugged, scraping her shoulder blades against the rough grain of the chair's wood frame. "I just wasn't feeling it, you know."

Teresa smirked and turned her attention to her girlfriend. Monica danced with abandon on the floor space designated for booty shaking. Monica loved to dance, Teresa not so much. Veronica was in Teresa's camp, so the two of them tended to sit around drinking and talking while women frolicked in front of them to the beat of music that was thankfully not too loud to inhibit conversation.

Despite Teresa's eyes remaining trained on Monica, her tone ensured Veronica that she was fully vested in this unwelcome discussion of her love life. Once a subject came up, Teresa didn't let it go until it had been thoroughly wrung out. So it wasn't unexpected when Teresa asked, "What does that mean? What didn't you feel?"

Veronica threw her head back to take a long slug of her

hard cider. It allowed her time to choose her words carefully. She started all this months ago with a simple comment, and now Teresa wouldn't let it go. A part of her knew that she didn't want Teresa to let it go. She needed to understand herself. The other part of her wanted to turn away and leave it all be. "He just wasn't right for me."

"Why?"

"He was kind of a jerk," Veronica lied.

"No, he wasn't. There was nothing wrong with him." Teresa turned to face her, eyes piercing even in the pulsing shadows and light of the club. She yanked Veronica's chair toward her, sliding abruptly so their foreheads bumped together. "You went out for like three weeks. I met him twice. That's a big deal. It tells me things were going well. And he was a nice guy. And he wasn't *Lane*."

"This isn't about, Lane," Veronica said coldly.

"Well, that we agree on. I don't think it is either. I think it's about something else." Teresa turned her head sharply away from Veronica toward the dance floor before swiveling it back and penetrating Veronica's gaze again.

Veronica gritted her teeth. Being forced to confront something she'd rather shove away brought out the anger in her. It didn't matter that she was the one to first broach the subject with Teresa months ago. When Teresa brought it up tonight, it took her out of the driver's seat. And that made Veronica crazy.

She took a slow sip of her drink and said casually, "I like men just fine, T."

"I don't doubt that. But thirty-five years of just one flavor, when you were born for more, might cause a bit of boredom."

Veronica had no desire to fight with Teresa. Lately, she was the best chance Veronica had to figure her shit out. Teresa was the ear she needed. So, she shoved her usual petulant reaction deep down in her chest and completely ignored the most important part of that statement, focusing instead on the exact math. "I haven't been a sexual being for my entire life. I didn't have my first crush until I was twelve. And I'm still thirty-four, thank you very much."

Teresa pierced her with a daring gaze. Veronica turned

away to study the dance floor with an intensity that practically radiated off her. She tried to think about all the ways she could occupy her mind without thinking of those words she'd uttered at this very table two days after Agnes and Helen's wedding.

Seeing her cousin's ex-wife just as happy—maybe happier—at her second wedding as at her first drove home a thought Veronica had been playing with for a long time. Could a person truly be as attracted to one gender as they were to the other? So many people doubted it. But Veronica had always known deep down that it was real. So real.

"Can we talk about this later?" Veronica asked.

Teresa's surprise acquiescence, in the form of a soft smile and a nod, allowed Veronica to relax for a moment. She leaned back and closely examined each person dancing on the slightly raised platform just a few feet away. A handful of women danced together in a way that was fun, not sexual. But the rest of the occupants were couples. Some were clearly longtime partners, their bodies smashed together in close embraces. Others were more tentative.

One couple snagged Veronica's attention. Clearly on a first or second date, they moved uneasily with one another, hands careful, eyes darting around rather than holding one another's intense gaze. Despite their discomfort, they were no less graceful, especially the young, stunning woman with short, dark hair and a perfectly angled face.

Veronica couldn't ignore the way her body swayed. She was short, her eyes level with her partner's collar bone. The woman would stand just below Veronica, their lips just inches from being perfectly aligned. Despite her stature, her amazing curves flowed and moved like a silk scarf blowing in the wind.

"See something you like?"

Veronica should have turned to Teresa and denied it. But she didn't. Because she couldn't. Eyes still pinned to the stunning woman, she let a tiny noise escape the back of her throat. She was too busy watching the dancer to pay much attention to Teresa's laughter.

****

Kaia had to hand it to Helen, she'd set up a good blind date. Lila seemed to be a great match. Conversation flowed like water through rapids as they compared jobs—both of which incited interest in storyteller and listener alike. Both women shared a love of dancing and moved on the floor as if they were velvet curtains intertwined in the elaborate ebb and flow from a cool breeze. To top it all off—she was easy on the eyes.

"Tell me about being a legal secretary. How did you decide to get into that?"

Lila's killer smile lit up the tiny round table they perched at. The sweat on her brow served as an indicator that their dancing gave her as much of a workout as it did Kaia. "I planned to be a lawyer, actually. Still do. But I didn't do so great on the LSAT the first time, and a pre-law professor of mine got me a job with the county prosecutor's office. He told me that in a few years, I'd be ready to retake it."

Kaia sipped her whiskey and water gingerly before responding. "Is that working out?"

Lila laughed. Her head flew back, exposing a long, sleek neck. "So far, no *bueno*. I've been so busy at work I haven't had time to study. I like my job, though. It's fascinating."

"I agree. I mean, you must see so much, every piece of paper that comes through the prosecutor's office. What I wouldn't give to have that kind of info for my podcast."

"Speaking of which, your job is pretty interesting, too. Do you like it?"

"Yeah. I mean, my new job, I like. The boring tech job I had before, not so much."

Lila lingered over a long sip of her wine, eyes roaming over Kaia above the rim of her glass. She set the drink down carefully. "How did you get the job with the podcast?"

Kaia traced the shape of Lila's lips with her gaze. "A friend from college, Heath, called me out of the blue one day. I knew about the show, of course. I've been a fan from the very beginning. I knew, like anyone who listens to the show, that Heath and Agnes started it together. But then Heath got the job as co-anchor of *True Crime Tonight*. He'd been hemming and hawing about taking the job because there was no way he could do it and the podcast because the podcast had become a full-time gig. But Agnes talked him in to taking the co-anchor gig. She wanted him to follow his dreams, but she insisted he find a replacement to help her out. So, he called me."

"To do the sound tech on the podcast?"

Kaia took another sip of her drink and looked away, eyelids fluttering. Talking about other people's high opinion of her stuck a knife in her gut. She remembered Heath's praise for her and the supreme confidence he expressed in her abilities made her want to crawl under the table. But she drew in a deep breath and plunged into the explanation, leaving the self-deprecation in the muddy pit where it belonged. "More than that, really. Agnes and Helen are starting a family. He wanted someone who could really help her with everything the way he did, and, you know, take some of the pressure off."

"And he thought of you to fill those big shoes."

Kaia shifted her gaze to concentrate on the wood grain of the table. "Yeah. I guess."

"Well, I think it sounds like Heath thinks quite highly of you."

A lifetime of turning away from compliments overrode politeness. Kaia glanced up from the table, but still avoided Lila's eyes. Instead, she glared at the dance floor as if it had offended her, concentrating on the new bodies there.

A woman, who'd been dancing on her own for a while, dragged two of her friends up the short step onto the raised platform and twirled with them into a spot directly in her line of sight. It quickly became apparent that two of the women were together. They tried to include their third wheel in the dancing, but the smoldering looks and touches between them gave it all away.

The extra didn't seem to mind. One of those women who oozed self-confidence. She wore a dress that appeared to be the base layer of a suit. It should have been out of place in a club, but the way it left her arms, and most of her toned legs, bare seemed to work just fine.

Elegant and powerful, the woman's sensual combination sent Kaia's libido shooting through the sky. Fortunately, Kaia's immense willpower took over to pull her gaze away from the dance floor and back to her date.

She flashed Lila her brightest smile and hoped the blatant gawking would go unnoticed. But Lila's own head was pivoted toward the dance floor. She, too, focused on the blonde on the dance floor. But instead of mirroring Kaia's sloppy expression of lust, Lila's face told a different story.

Eyes squinted and head forward, Lila appeared to be examining the dancer as if she were a specimen under a microscope. "I think that's...wow...it can't be."

Kaia sat back, her gaze following Lila's back to the woman whose incredible figure was on display as she circled her hips in an undeniably sexy way. "You know her?"

"Of her. She's the most terrifying defense attorney in town. They call her the tigress."

Kaia chuckled. She could find nothing scary about the soft smile painted on the woman's lips or the way her head leaned back, exposing a tender neck, smooth and perfectly kissable.

The stranger's lush throat abruptly disappeared from Kaia's view as the woman brought her head down. Even in the oscillating lights of the club, her bright blue eyes were clear as they made direct contact with Kaia, paralyzing her entire body.

In that brief, intense moment of connection, Lila, who felt a hundred miles away, spoke the name of the dancer. Her voice echoed in Kaia's head with a shattering surety. "Yeah. That's definitely her. That's Veronica Turner."

Chapter Three

"So, um," Agnes folded her hands together on the scrub pine table. "I have to admit I didn't read the entire research brief you sent."

Kaia counted at least four yawns and three eye rubs since Agnes welcomed Kaia into her dining room no more than ten minutes ago. "I don't blame you. It was pretty long, and um, you looked…tired."

"I am." Agnes went for eye rub number four, pressing her palm to her lid. "There's a lot of paperwork to do, plus things to set up for the home visit. And Helen hasn't had a break from constant surgeries in weeks." Agnes dropped her hand and a large, genuine smile spread across her face. "But it's all going to be worth it when we have our baby."

Warmth spread through Kaia, a feeling of mutual understanding. The exciting stress of a new life being delivered to your hands created a constant sensation in her chest. But she would never vocalize her empathy, since she wasn't sure everyone would feel the comparison of her situation to Agnes's was appropriate.

"So…would you mind summarizing?"

Kaia chuckled at Agnes's rueful expression. She'd come over to review her research on Jessica French the night before their interview. She shouldn't be surprised that Agnes hadn't read the entire fourteen-page dossier she'd sent hours ago. "Of course. No problem."

Agnes settled back in her chair, eyes wide, mouth turned into a half smile, the perfect audience save for her potential to slip into sleep at any moment.

"Okay." Kaia pushed the button on her tablet, lighting it up. She didn't need to scan the document, everything in it was filed away in her brain. A sense of stage fright always ran through her when all the attention—even that of just one person—focused on her. The laptop served as a crutch. It allowed her to look away and focus on the words coming out of her mouth. "Let's start with Jessica's finances."

"She inherited her money, right?"

"Yes, but it's not endlessly accessible."

"I know. That's why Veronica is working for free."

"So that's how a young attorney, not attached to a big firm, landed such an incredibly rich client? I mean, I would expect someone like Jessica French to have a giant team of super expensive attorneys."

"Well, there are kind of two answers to that," Agnes said. "The first is that Veronica has an amazing reputation. She used to be with a big firm. When she was brand new they threw her a murder case that was considered unwinnable. The guy was innocent—at least I think so. But the entire system was stacked against him. Anyway, that's a whole podcast." Agnes flashed a smile. "But Veronica got him off. So they gave her more and more cases like that. She won them all. Then one day she decided to go off on her own. She said it was so she could take the cases she wanted, not the ones assigned to her. She always tells people that she only takes innocent clients. I'm pretty sure there's more to the story, but I don't know it."

Kaia understood a willingness to leave her security and strike out on her own because she'd done it herself. But despite that experience, there seemed to be little else that she and Veronica had in common. "So, she became a firm of one?"

"Yeah. I mean she has staff people and contracted investigators and such. But she's the only attorney. There are a couple of other independent attorneys she teams up with from time to time. But not this time. She's on her own. She's kind of a gambler. She's only going to get paid if she gets Jessica off. Thanks to that trust."

Kaia leaned forward, her elbows propped on the table. "So, you wanna hear what I found out about the trust?"

Agnes matched her pose, their heads coming together conspiratorially as if they were plotting the demise of the government. "Of course I do."

"Jessica set up a trust that prevents her money from being accessible if she is out of commission."

"Meaning what?"

Kaia shrugged. "In a coma, on a ventilator, in jail, I guess."

"So she made her own money inaccessible? She did this to herself?"

"She did. Though I'm sure she never imagined she would end up in jail without a penny to her name, not even bail."

Agnes harrumphed. "I'm sure she didn't."

"Nope. But the paperwork is ironclad. So she's stuck. Thank goodness for Veronica, I guess."

Agnes replied with a low hum emanating from her throat.

"Can I ask you a question?"

"Sure," Agnes said.

Kaia twisted her fingers together. "Understanding that Jessica is broke at the moment, it still seems as though a lot of lawyers would be willing to take a gamble like that, given how much Jessica is worth when her money isn't tied up."

"Probably." Agnes blinked her eyes and kept her focus on Kaia as if waiting for sense to come out of her mouth.

Kaia released a massive breath, the wind from the action causing an errant lock of hair to fly around her forehead.

Agnes lit up, her mouth turning up at the corners. "Veronica has an amazing reputation."

This still baffled Kaia. Jessica French was the sole heiress to a massive, and still growing, fortune from one of the oldest textile companies in the western U.S., her name so powerful that her husband took it when they got married, leaving behind a life of anonymity to bare the French mark.

Jessica's name was so well known that in the last few years she started a line of throw pillows with her signature stamped across them. This fun little side project blossomed based solely on her name.

Jessica French broke seemed impossible to most people, but Kaia knew better. "I still think other attorneys would want to get in on the potential windfall."

Agnes held up two fingers. "One, she's known to be a nightmare of a human being. Two, no one else thinks she'll get off, innocent or not."

"Because of reason number one," Kaia said.

"Yup."

"So Veronica really is taking a gamble?" The sheer courage of this action invoked a respect Kaia could not deny.

Agnes shook her head. "Not in her mind. She knows she'll win."

That kind of confidence when faced with what most people considered an unwinnable case boggled Kaia's mind.

"In fact, she's hoping to get Jessica out of the charges before it even goes to trial. She wants the public to demand Jessica's release."

With Jessica French's reputation as the most narcissistic, unlikable human in the Bay Area, the idea of making her into a people's cause seemed like a pipe dream.

Agnes spoke as though she read Kaia's mind. "She can do it." Agnes's voice lowered as if her next words were spoken to herself and not to Kaia at all. "And I'm going to help. I owe her."

"So, um, she helped with Helen's thing, right?" Kaia bit her lower lip as soon as she asked, anxiety coursing through her. Regardless of the discomfort of the subject, she felt compelled to bring it up.

"Yeah. Veronica is Malcolm's cousin. Adopted."

While this probably should have been obvious given that Helen's ex-husband, Malcolm, was Black and Veronica was white, it didn't necessarily mean anything to Kaia. Because of her own family make-up, she made no assumptions.

Something else about the revelation intrigued Kaia though. "Veronica was adopted?"

"Yep. By Malcolm's aunt Florence and Uncle Mike. She was abandoned just after birth at the hospital where Mike worked. Anyway, the family is really tight and so Helen has known Veronica since she first started dating Malcolm. Helen and Malcolm were in high school and she was in college."

Kaia quickly did the math. She knew Veronica was young for how far she'd come in her career, but she had to at least be in her mid-thirties. Since Helen and Agnes had both recently leaped over the thirty threshold—a milestone Kaia was still five years from hitting—that would be about right.

Agnes ran a hand through her wavy, brunette hair. "Anyway, she's family."

"How did she take it when she found out her cousin's ex-wife was with a woman?" This question sat itself on Kaia's mind and refused to leave, spurred on by the smoldering look she'd shared with Veronica in the club two days ago.

"I wasn't there for that conversation. But Helen said it was pretty smooth. No drama. I just assumed Veronica was as accepting as the rest of the family, until our wedding."

Kaia's curiosity spiked, like the heartbeat on an EKG. "What happened at your wedding?"

"Nothing happened, she was just weird."

Something inside her gut forced Kaia to pursue this line of questioning. "Weird how?"

Agnes shrugged. "I don't really know. I just remember discussing it with Helen and Malcolm. Like she was acting strange, you know?"

No, Kaia didn't know. But she wanted to. What did that mean, acting strange? What was happening inside her head? And did it have anything to do with the moment they'd exchanged at the club?

These questions flew through her brain and forced another out of her mouth. "So, um, she's straight though, right?"

Agnes shrugged. "I mean, she's only been with men that I know of. But that doesn't mean anything."

"Okay, but she never told you that she was anything other than straight?"

Agnes gazed at Kaia with an expression of pure curiosity. "Why? What are you worried about? I mean, she's not a homophobe or anything."

Kaia swiveled away from Agnes, her eyes pinned to a large wedding photo of Agnes and Helen that hung on the cream-colored wall. "No. I get that. I just…wondered about her, that's all. She seems pretty intense."

The click of the deadbolt being snapped open brought

an end to their conversation. Helen was home. They would no doubt shift the topic to her job or the baby. But before that happened, even as she rose from her seat, Agnes said to Kaia, "Don't worry. Her bark is worse than her bite. Deep down, she's a sweet lady."

Never in her life had Kaia doubted anything more.

****

"The most important thing is that you be likable," Veronica said. "Do you think that's even remotely possible?" Sure, snark wasn't usually the most effective approach. Even though she'd never read one, Veronica was sure those stupid instruction books on how to talk to difficult people advised against it. Of course, most people she knew read those books to deal with her.

Predictably, Jessica reacted by ignoring any suggestion that everyone in the world didn't already love her. "I'll tell the truth."

"Okay, yes. But let's talk about exactly how you're going to tell the truth."

Unwilling to ever forfeit her reigning title as Drama Queen, Jessica let out a massive sigh. "I'm going to explain that I didn't kill him. I came home and Gregory was gone."

"And there was enough blood soaked into your carpet to give the medical examiner a reason to determine that its source, a.k.a Gregory, must be dead. You know Agnes is going to ask you about that."

"Well, tell her not to." Jessica folded her arms over her chest, which made the pumpkin orange material of her loose top wrinkle awkwardly. The woman who'd once walked a runway must hate every moment of this fashion disaster.

"It doesn't work that way."

"Why the hell not? You said this person owes you."

Certain no one had ever bothered to explain to Jessica the difference between a favor and a demand, Veronica chose to once again ignore the more obnoxious part of her client's statement. "She will probably ask about the blood."

"You know I don't have an answer."

The biggest hole in this case—the unexplained presence of Gregory's blood coupled with the even more confounding absence of his body—stared at them like a yawning hole they must somehow traverse. Veronica believed in conquering the largest obstacle first. That methodology kept her undefeated in murder trials so far. It also didn't hurt that she only took on innocent clients—the advantage of being in private practice.

"Well, we need to come up with one. In the meantime, I'll make sure we avoid that question." Veronica raised one eyebrow. "For now."

Jessica narrowed her eyes into thin slits, like the opening for a robot laser beam in an old sci-fi movie. Her long, Roman nose created a slide for her evil thoughts to travel down on their way to Veronica's beating heart. The intimidation may have worked with everyone else in Jessica's life, but it wouldn't work with Veronica. She glared back, the laser jets attached to her own eyes far more powerful.

Jessica suddenly squeezed her eyes shut. When they opened again, they were focused on the table in front of her. "So, what the hell are we going to talk about?"

"You. We're going to talk about you." Veronica took in a deep breath and tried to breathe through the thick air of the dank, windowless room. The battered table between them seemed to peel beneath her hands and Jessica's tortured gaze. "We're going to start at the beginning. Talk about your life. All the hard parts."

Jessica's head shot up; her chin practically pointed at the ceiling.

"I mean it," Veronica warned. "Leave nothing that makes you look sympathetic out. That includes your asshole dad and your gold-digging husband."

Jessica's chin quivered, her lips pressed together, shooting tiny lines down toward her chin. Veronica let out a sigh of relief. In most circumstances, the silence of a person about to be interviewed might be considered a bad sign. But with Jessica, it became a welcome reprieve from her constant petulance.

Veronica sat with her back to the wall, so when the

heavy metal door swung open opposite her it didn't create a reaction. Jessica, on the other hand, jolted, her entire body nearly leaping out of the creaky wooden chair.

The corrections officer spoke in a clear and even tone. "The remaining two approved guests have arrived."

Veronica matched the woman's intensely serious expression and nodded. "Thank you."

Agnes stepped through the doorway, passing the guard like a wispy ghost. Pale skin framed dark, matte brown eyes. If Veronica had to guess, Agnes hadn't slept well in days. She wanted to hold an interrogation of her own to get to the bottom of this disturbing change in appearance.

But this wasn't the time or place, so she swallowed back her questions and nodded at Agnes. She stretched her arm and pointed to one of two empty chairs squeezed around the small, rickety table.

The remaining seat at the table loomed large and spacious by comparison, specially prepared with all the equipment Agnes's new tech person would surely be lugging along in mind. As Agnes lowered herself into her own seat, Veronica refocused on the door, her hand extended toward the empty space designated for the person whose name she'd already forgotten.

A tiny woman covered in gear slid through the door and completely avoided her gaze. But Veronica watched every step she took from the doorway to the seat. She closely examined the woman's face and her perfectly proportioned body.

No question about it, this was the irresistible woman from the club.

Chapter Four

Kaia managed to keep her gaze fenced in, staying firmly in her small area packed with equipment. Her eyes bounced from her laptop to the microphone, to the tablet beside it, anything to avoid looking at Veronica. Kaia squirmed in her hard seat. Despite hers being the largest space at the table, Veronica was still far too close, her presence like a radiator spewing hot steam in a tiny, stuffy room—uncomfortable and inescapable.

"Let's talk about how you and Gregory met," Agnes said to Jessica, a big reporter smile on her face.

The woman stared at Agnes, her piercing eyes peering out over rough orange fabric with the best resting bitch face Kaia had ever seen. "He was an intern at the company."

Kaia assumed Jessica would try to play it off that Gregory had been a regular employee. That's what she'd told a magazine reporter when they got engaged. Instead she stormed into the conversation with the bare truth. Just as Kaia had discovered in her research, Gregory was a twenty-year-old intern when he met the thirty-five year old heiress.

"And did you fall in love right away?" Agnes asked.

Jessica blinked. "What are you asking me?"

"You know," Agnes said. "Tell me about your courtship."

Jessica snorted. "What are you from, the eighteen century?" She glared across the table at Veronica. "Who the hell talks like that?"

"My very good friend and the woman who is saving your ass. Answer the question." After verbally whipping her client, Veronica turned to Kaia. "You aren't going to use that are you?"

Veronica's hand landed on Kaia's forearm. Kaia was using that arm to hold the mic, so she couldn't pull it away on instinct as she'd wished. Her head snapped to the side. Veronica stared her down. "Are you?"

Kaia managed to shake her head.

"Good. Tell them how long you dated Gregory." Veronica's hand slipped off Kaia's arm as she issued her demand to Jessica.

Kaia turned to her laptop, attempting to completely ignore everything but her job.

"It was like three or four months before we got engaged," Jessica said. "I don't remember exactly."

"And?" Agnes prompted.

"And I asked him," Jessica said harshly.

"Really?" Agnes's voice rang with curiosity. The news hit Kaia unexpectedly as well. It hadn't come up in her research about the relationship between the heiress and her talentless husband.

"Yeah. So? I mean, didn't you ask a woman to marry you?" Jessica asked.

Without a hint of anger, Agnes answered. "I did."

"So, if lesbians can do it, why can't I?"

"Jessica." The single word erupted from Veronica's throat like a growl.

Kaia glanced up, her gaze meeting Agnes's eye—focused, amused, and completely unshaken. "What about the ring?" Agnes nodded at Jessica's now bare finger. Despite its absence, the memory of the massive rock seen in every image of Jessica plastered all over local news remained. Every picture of Jessica in the paper, every quick paparazzi image on television featured that enormous ring. "Did you pick it out together afterward, or what?" Agnes asked.

"I bought it my damn self. Is that what you want to hear?" Jessica said.

Agnes nodded. Yes. Clearly, it was exactly what she wanted to hear.

"I don't see how any of this is relevant," Veronica interjected.

Kaia bit her tongue, fighting back the urge to remind Veronica that it was she who'd insisted Jessica talk about this subject. But despite the desire to serve as Veronica's personal playback machine, talking to Veronica sat very last on Kaia's to-do list.

"I think the details of Jessica and Gregory's relationship are extremely relevant," Agnes said. "We want to tell the listeners the story of them as a couple. It will help to create a bigger picture when we get to the mystery of how Gregory died."

A deep pause impregnated the room. Kaia allowed her gaze to travel around the table, taking in all three women, their postures giving away so much of the interaction. Agnes leaned back in her chair, relaxed and at home, which might not have been entirely true, but she was a professional interviewer and knew how to fake it with the best of them. Jessica's dipped eyebrows and pressed-thin lips gave away her anger, which seemed to be her usual state. And Veronica, with her narrowed eyes and flared nostrils appeared every bit the fierce attorney whispered about in bars.

Veronica finally leaned back, the clunking metal folding chair giving out a pained groan. She slowly folded her arms over her chest. "Tell her," she commanded.

A long, deep, and highly dramatic breath left Jessica's lungs. "He was all for getting married, too. But he was broke. I paid for everything. So what? I'm rich."

"But not anymore, right?" Agnes said.

Jessica's face turned the deepest shade of mauve. Her eyes nearly popped as far away from her face as the vein in her forehead. "What did you just say to me?"

"I mean," Agnes said, her tone completely calm. "That you obviously didn't have anything to gain with Gregory's death. I just want to clarify that for our listeners."

The thick tension in the room released its hold like air escaping a balloon. "Oh."

Veronica inserted herself in the showdown between the two women. "See, she's got your best interests in mind, Jessica. Just answer the question."

Jessica held a small paper cup—that presumably held the same watered-down coffee perched in front of Kaia—in both her cuffed hands and stared into its contents. "Just like you said. I don't have any money."

"Where did it all go?"

"It still exists. It's just tied up." Jessica brought the cup to her lips, made a huge play of blowing on it, even though there was no way in hell it was a degree past lukewarm. Then, gingerly took a slow sip.

With the patience of a saint, Agnes continued to pull teeth. "Tied up how?"

Like a tired tortoise, Jessica moved her hands to the table and rolled her shoulders. Another three measured breaths later, she spoke. "I made arrangements that if anything happened to me while I was still alive, the money would go into a locked trust. No one can get to it, not even me, until I die. And then it goes to my niece, or I become…ya know…better or whatever, and I get the money back."

"What constitutes something happening to you?" Agnes asked, a soft smile playing on her lips.

Veronica jumped in again. "The document specifies any event that keeps Jessica from effectively managing her own affairs. This includes everything from say a surgery or coma to kidnapping."

"To jail," Agnes said.

"Yes. To jail," Veronica confirmed.

"So, it's all completely stuck as long as you're in here, even for bail?" Agnes asked.

"No," Veronica said. "We could use it for bail, because I could get a loan and then pay it off as soon as she's out and able to use the money, but I can't get the damn judge to give her bail."

Kaia knew that wasn't strange for someone accused of first-degree murder, especially someone with the means to flee. She also knew there was an exception to the rule that locked up Jessica's money. Because she had failed to tell Agnes about it when she'd given her the rundown of her research, she had no choice but to voice it now.

"There is one exception." Every eye in the room turned to Kaia. Veronica kept her own gaze on the dingy wall opposite them. "There is money that can be used for the upkeep of the dog," Kaia said.

"The dog?" Agnes asked. "The dog that's at my house right now?"

"You have Pookie?" Jessica's body shifted toward Agnes, her eyes round and bright.

"Yeah. I…Malcolm is my…he's a good friend of my wife, and he asked us to take care of her. But I swear my wife and I didn't know anything about any money."

"How is she? Is she okay?" Thin and desperate, Jessica's voice barely made it across the table.

"She's good. She gets along great with our two dogs. She's very happy. I swear."

"Wait." Veronica held up her hand. "Agnes, are you saying you don't know anything about the money for Pookie? Haven't you heard from the trust attorney?"

Agnes shook her head.

There was a beat before Veronica leaned back in her chair. "Well, I'm sure you will soon."

Something prickled at the back of Kaia's neck. She wasn't entirely certain what it was. But she decided to chalk it up to the fact that Veronica stared at her with a hair-raising intensity.

****

Veronica craved more time with the beautiful, young woman who dramatically snagged her attention that night at the club. The moment Kaia walked into the stuffy little room at the jail, she was determined to make it happen.

Fortunately, Agnes had a free afternoon, so convincing her to accept Veronica's offer to buy lunch was relatively simple. Kaia, on the other hand, tried to slip away, which would have completely defeated the purpose of the invitation.

Veronica pushed the right buttons by implying that the lunch was imperative to continuing on the Jessica French project. That power was handed to her halfway through the interview. The image of a diamond practically appeared above Jessica's head as she spoke. Her story held incredible promise, especially for a burgeoning true crime podcast dependent on capturing the public's interest and wrapping it up in intrigue. Veronica went from begging Agnes and Kaia to feature Jessica on their podcast last week to the storytellers chomping at the bit to air the sordid tale.

Clearly a professional, Kaia took the bait. Veronica didn't feel the least bit guilty about it. Nor did she mind crossing about eight lines when she told Kaia, "Tell me about your personal life," within two minutes of ordering lunch.

It was important to order before asking uncomfortable questions, because then people would be less likely to get up and leave. Kaia nearly ruined that by not ordering anything other than an iced tea. But Veronica didn't let that stop her from moving forward with her plan to find out more about Kaia.

Kaia gaped at her. Her intriguing lips wide open, she stared hard across the table. Unfazed, Veronica stared back, waiting.

"Veronica's kinda like this," Agnes told Kaia.

"So I see," Kaia replied.

"You want me to tell you my story first?"

She might have said it half in jest, but Kaia took the bait. "Okay." She folded her arms over her chest. "Go ahead."

Veronica ignored the smirk on Agnes's lips and kept her gaze on Kaia. "I'm adopted."

This confession usually had a big impact on people, when she chose to tell it. But, to her disappointment, Kaia just nodded.

"Agnes told you?"

Kaia nodded again.

Veronica practically melted into her chair. Her big entrance ruined, she tried to think of what she could say next to intrigue the young woman. "My parents couldn't conceive, and they kind of adopted me by accident. So I grew up an only child. That probably doesn't surprise you. It doesn't surprise anyone. Apparently, I act like an only child." She grinned.

The edge of Kaia's mouth ticked up ever so slightly, but otherwise she stayed perfectly still.

"I bet you're one of at least three or four, am I right?" Veronica asked.

Kaia shook her head. "This is supposed to be about you."

Veronica's love of challenge jumped to the surface and she continued. "Anyway, big family though. Twelve first cousins, including Malcolm, of course. Lots of fun. I was the one in charge of all the games we played, even though I'm not the oldest."

"No one ever accused you of being a follower, Veronica," Agnes quipped.

Kaia's expression remained blank. So Veronica went further. "I was almost the valedictorian at my high school. Literally second. Then I went to Stanford. I graduated Summa Cum Laude in three and half years."

Nothing changed on Kaia's face, so Veronica tried again. "I was in the top ten of my law class, too."

Kaia finally spoke, but her question threw Veronica for a loop. "What were you like in college?"

"What do you mean?" Veronica rarely expressed confusion. But in this case, she couldn't help it. What the hell kind of question was that? Why didn't she ask about Veronica's other accomplishments, or how it felt to be such a rising star at such a young age?

"What did you do for fun? What kind of friends did you have? Did you have a job in college?" Kaia asked.

Veronica nearly stuttered, but she caught herself and clamped her mouth shut. Agnes answered one of the questions for her. "Malcolm told me that Veronica had a side job all through school—modeling."

"Modeling?" Kaia's eyebrows rose. Her eyes traveled slowly down Veronica's torso—everything above the table. "I can see that."

Veronica burned. The quiet, shy woman just made a blatant and sexually aggressive move. Veronica nearly leapt over the table. But Kaia just sat there, quietly waiting for an answer.

"Yes. Modeling. I was good at it. Made enough money to seriously cut down on student loans. It's also how I initially met Jessica. We modeled together. What about you, Kaia? Where did you go to school?"

Kaia shook her head so hard her short hair swung around her head. "We're still on you."

The distinct sound of an amused snort came from

Agnes, but Veronica ignored it and kept her focus on Kaia. "I quit modeling when I went to law school. No time. No time for anything, really."

"Even dating?" Agnes asked, one brow raised. She knew very little about Veronica's love life. Few people did, and Veronica liked it that way.

Veronica's love life featured a string of failures reaching back to high school. She hated getting into it. Fortunately, the server returned with their meals and gave her a temporary reprieve from having to deal with that mess.

Veronica waited until every plate of food and glass or mug of drink was carefully placed in its proper position on the linoleum table. At that point the expectation of her answer demanded attention again. She intended to answer, but only in a way that would lead back to her intended subject—Kaia. "My internship in law school was so intense, I barely had time to eat, let alone sleep. But it was worth it because I landed an amazing job at a firm as soon as I passed the bar. That led to me being one of the most successful defense attorneys in the county under forty. And now I work for myself. That's my story. Tell me yours?"

Kaia fiddled with her iced tea, swiveling the ceramic mug in her hand. The absence of a plate of food in front of her conspicuous as Agnes gratefully dug into a massive salad and Veronica's gourmet sandwich awaited her attention. Why had Kaia refused to eat? She had to be hungry. It was nearly two o'clock. The woman was a healthy weight, she obviously ate at some point in her day. Why not now? Why not in this nice restaurant?

Kaia glanced at her phone, then up at Agnes. Veronica knew that face. Kaia's expression, lips turned down, eyes squinted. Kaia was trapped. She rode to the jail with Agnes. Now, desperate to leave, she couldn't ask for a ride home from her still-dining boss without being rude.

"Um." Kaia's gaze flickered between Veronica and the polished tabletop. "I met Heath in school. He was doing a mentoring program and I was in the pod of students he worked with. When he needed to find someone to help Agnes out—"

"Partner with me," Agnes interjected.

"Um, yeah. He asked me."

"And?" Veronica prompted.

"And, I was bored at my old job and excited about the opportunity, so I said yes. And thankfully, Agnes gave me the job."

"Partnership," Agnes said again.

Kaia nodded and shrugged. "That's about it."

"What else?" Veronica had never been so dissatisfied with a grilling in her life. Usually people rambled on about all their personal shit when she was trying to get something very specific out of them. Here she wanted to know every little detail about Kaia, and she was getting nothing.

"There's nothing else." Kaia's tone reflected a clear level of annoyance.

"Love life, hobbies, come on, tell me something real about yourself."

"I'd rather not." The cold look in Kaia's eyes, which were now firmly planted on Veronica's face, told her she wouldn't be getting what she wanted. And Veronica hated that.

"What about something simple?"

Kaia sighed. "Like what?"

"Why aren't you eating lunch?"

Kaia's cold demeanor suddenly changed. Her face softened, and she rubbed her forehead with the palm of her hand.

"She has a special diet," Agnes said.

Kaia lifted her head. "I have Celiac disease. I prefer not to eat out until I get my dog." She turned to Agnes and smiled.

"Do you know when that will be?" Agnes asked.

"I got an email the other day, it sounds like a few months."

Whatever this personal conversation was, Veronica wanted in on it. She hated being left out like this. "Explain," she demanded. Both women pivoted their heads to stare at her, and she knew she'd been too harsh again. Damn. "I mean, what is Celiac disease, and what does it have to do with a dog?"

"You don't know what Celiac disease is?" Agnes probably

didn't mean any harm in asking. Her surprise most likely just got the best of her. But the way the question was phrased chafed at Veronica.

Kaia's sweet response stopped Veronica from saying something snarky to her friend. "Lots of people don't know what it is. It's an autoimmune reaction to gluten."

Veronica knew at least half a dozen people who claimed that they couldn't eat gluten, but none of them had ever used the word "autoimmune" and her teasing them about not eating bread seemed completely out of place now. Instead, she schooled her features, rested her chin on her hands and said, "Tell me more."

Kaia shrugged, her round shoulders briefly hiding what Veronica considered to be a fully kissable neck. That she'd never thought that about any other woman's neck in the history of forever seemed irrelevant at the moment. "Ingesting gluten makes my immune system attack my small intestine. It causes a lot of trouble, including malnutrition. Not that I look malnourished anymore." She blushed the most delightful shade of red. "Anyway. It's really hard to avoid cross contamination. So I'm getting a service dog to detect gluten in my food."

"Wait. This is a thing? A service dog for this?" Veronica rarely burst out her surprise, but she was completely caught up.

"It's a disability," Agnes said. "It's in the ADA."

Veronica knew a lot about the Americans with Disabilities Act. She'd done a ton of research on it once for a client. She knew that eating was a covered life function, meaning that if a person couldn't safely eat, they were considered disabled. Suddenly, the severity of Kaia's disease hit her. This was not her friend, Jill, who thought avoiding gluten would help her lose weight, this was a woman with a serious medical disorder, one that kept her from eating at restaurants and required her to explain herself all the time.

"I'm sorry." Veronica hadn't used those two words in earnest in a very long time. But they tasted sweet and right now.

"It's fine. I really need to get going." Kaia stood. "I can take the bus."

Agnes dropped her fork. "No. I'll drive you."

Kaia waved her hand as she walked away. "It's good. Finish your lunch."

And just like that, the gorgeous, intriguing, mysterious Kaia was gone.

Chapter Five

The door swung open to reveal Agnes's wife, Helen—stunning and happier than ever. "Veronica! This is a surprise."

Three dogs of varying sizes leapt at her ankles as she shoved her way into the small condo. "I hope you're not cooking."

"Um. We were just getting started."

"Well, put a lid on it. I brought Chinese." She hefted a white plastic bag with red writing, swinging it precariously close to Helen's nose.

"Oh, okay." Kind and accommodating, as always, Helen led her into the kitchen where Agnes stood at the cutting board, knife held over an onion. "Look. Veronica brought us dinner."

Agnes carefully set the knife down and plastered on a smile. "Awesome. Thanks, Veronica."

"No problem." She dropped the plastic bag on the kitchen island and slipped onto one of four barstools.

Helen gathered plates and utensils, while Agnes took a pair of scissors and gingerly cut open the tied plastic before pulling the cardboard containers out.

Veronica chuckled as Agnes glared at the plastic bag held between her thumb and forefinger like it was radioactive. Then she shoved it into a paper bag and mumbled about finding a way to recycle it.

Once all three women had full plates and were settled at the island perched on bar stools, Veronica—at the guest position on the end—started the conversation lightly. "How goes the adoption drama? Is my friend, Erika, helping you out?"

"Erika is amazing," Agnes gushed. "Thanks again for finding her."

Veronica hadn't really "found" Erika at all. They'd gone to law school together. Erika went into family law while Veronica took the gritty route to murder and injustice.

"No problem. What's the word?"

Agnes and Helen exchanged a glance, their wide grins giving away the nature of the news they had to share. Helen turned back to Veronica. "We're not telling the families yet, mostly because we don't want them to freak out if it falls through. But there is some really exciting news."

Veronica stuck her fork in a piece of orange chicken. "Tell me about it." She would never admit her nervousness as she waited for their answer. But she couldn't help the quiver in her stomach. She dragged the chicken around her plate, spreading the orange sauce across the porcelain.

A lot rode on this seemingly benign conversation. Veronica had a big, loving family, but few genuine friends outside of Teresa. Even though their original connection was through family, Veronica had come to think of Agnes and Helen as true friends. If they confided in her something they were keeping from everyone else, it validated her perception of their relationship.

"There's a little girl in foster care right now, and we may get to adopt her." Helen's voice became a tiny squeal at the end of the sentence.

Veronica set her fork down and took in a deep breath. "Wow. Tell me about her."

Agnes jumped in then. "She just turned two. She's beyond beautiful. She was born addicted to drugs, has special needs, and we want her. We want her so bad."

Veronica smiled and told them the exact truth. "I think you'll be the perfect parents for her."

Jessica's tiny dog jumped up on Veronica's heel, dragging its sharp talons along her skin. She stared down at it, wondering if it had any clue how rich it was. "So, things are going well with this one?" She pointed to the small terrorist with pointy ears and a pert nose.

"To be honest, she's a little much," Helen admitted. "We're hoping you can get Jessica out of jail before the baby comes."

"I will."

"No doubt." Agnes raised her glass of tea toward Veronica.

"With your help." Veronica glared pointedly at Agnes.

Agnes laughed. "That's not our goal. Our goal is the truth."

Veronica rolled her eyes.

"Besides," Agnes added. "I'm going to be on the sidelines a lot. Kaia's your girl. She'll do a great job. I have so much faith in her."

Glad the conversation had naturally turned to Kaia, Veronica hoped it helped her achieve the true purpose of this visit—to get reconnaissance on the beautiful sound tech. "About that."

Helen and Agnes turned to her in unison. Agnes dropped her fork dramatically. "The show or Kaia?"

Veronica sat up, her back straight, her chin held high. "Kaia."

Helen set her own utensil down with a little more grace. "What about her?"

Veronica leaned back in her seat, the picture of casual self-composure. "Tell me about her. What's she like?"

Agnes mirrored Veronica and sat back casually. She glanced at Helen before piercing Veronica with her gaze. "She's very smart and extremely competent."

"And sweet. Very, very sweet," Helen added.

Veronica cocked her head. "She seems kind of shy."

"She's a little quiet, yeah," Agnes said.

"Why?" Veronica tipped her head, practically resting her cheek on her shoulder. She found that people opened up more when she looked curious and unassuming.

"I don't know. Why are people shy?" Agnes extended her arm toward Veronica. "Why are people incredibly nosey and invasive?"

Veronica blasted a grin at her. "I was born this way."

"Maybe she was born shy."

Helen held up her hands. "Okay. This conversation is getting weird. What do you really want to know, Veronica?"

"Can't I just ask about someone?" The innocent act wasn't working as well on these two as she'd hoped. She should have known better. Not even a casual acquaintance of hers would believe she was interested in something without a motive of some kind. Innocence just wasn't her thing.

Agnes pursed her lips. "You want to know about her, you can ask her yourself."

"Unless," Helen said, "you want to know something even you wouldn't ask someone you don't know very well."

Veronica pushed out a breath and resigned herself to the knowledge that she was about to expose her true mission. In a way, it was a weight lifted. She needed to come out with it and tell someone her thoughts. And she'd chosen Helen and Agnes to be those someones the minute she ordered that takeout.

"Is she bi, like you guys, or pan or whatever?"

Rather than look at her friends, Veronica spent the long pause staring at Jessica's tiny dog. It had given up its quest to jump up her leg and was now curled in a ball at her feet.

Finally, Agnes cleared her throat. "Um. No, she identifies as lesbian."

Veronica's eyes left the sleeping canine and traveled slowly back up to Agnes. "Really?"

"Yeah, why?" Agnes's eyes flashed with fierce protectiveness.

Veronica knew she should put Agnes at ease. Reassure her, yet again, that she wasn't judging anyone's sexuality. Far from it. Her own internal struggle sat at the heart of all of her words.

But how did a grown-ass woman reveal her questions? Shouldn't she have figured this out by now? Remembering that she didn't care what anyone thought about her, she squared her shoulders and asked, "How did you know you were bisexual?"

Another excruciatingly long pause followed. But this time, Veronica didn't avoid her friend's gaze. She stared right into those bright eyes and waited.

But it wasn't Agnes who answered. Instead, Helen leaned forward to get a better look at Veronica. "For me, it was when I developed a major crush on a girl a few weeks after I had one on a guy. It felt the same, the desire, I mean."

"But you were young, right?"

Agnes placed her hand over Veronica's, her expression suddenly soft. "Honey, age isn't important. You wanna tell us why you're asking?"

Veronica's tongue roamed her mouth, which was suddenly parched. She reached for her glass of water and took a healthy swig. When there was enough moisture for speech, she took in a deep breath and told her truth. "I have a serious crush on Kaia."

This time the pregnant pause in the room was actually painful. Veronica wished one of the dogs would at least yelp or bark or something, but a quick scan of the area showed all three completely passed out. The worthless bums.

"We hear you." Helen reached across Agnes to add her touch as well.

Veronica's throat tightened as if she'd just eaten shellfish. She suffered the same sensation the first time she gave an opening statement in court. "You think I'm crazy."

"No way," Agnes said quickly. "No way. We're one hundred percent here for you."

The idea that she'd just done something incredibly significant slammed into Veronica. She couldn't really be admitting that she was something other than she'd always claimed to be, could she? Was this really happening? At her age?

Then there was the deepest, truest question to face. Wasn't that exactly why she'd come here? To confess this very thing?

Helen got up and walked around the kitchen island. She bent down and disappeared from Veronica's sight for a minute. When she reappeared, she held a bottle of red wine and a corkscrew. "Let's talk."

****

Lila was a truly gorgeous woman. The way her hair cascaded over her shoulders and kissed the tops of her breasts was intoxicating. Kaia didn't know how well they meshed yet, but she certainly wanted to find out.

"Thanks for meeting me at such a weird time of day." Lila sipped her coffee gingerly.

Kaia held her own mug close to her on the small round table. "Ten isn't so weird." The sun struck their spot, the best little corner of the coffee shop, tucked against a floor-to-ceiling window that looked out on Market Street. "I work strange hours."

"Me too. I get away whenever there isn't some sort of legal emergency or court thing. Though, uh, I don't know why I picked this place to meet. I feel a little odd here." Lila scanned the front counter quickly. "I served the owner with a subpoena once."

"Awkward."

"Yeah. Awkward. But the coffee is so good." She took another sip as if to demonstrate.

"Location's not bad either." Kaia gestured with her coffee toward the window. It provided a dramatic view of the Ferry Building towering at the end of the street like an ancient sentinel watching over the Bay.

Lila swiveled her head to follow Kaia's gaze. "You know that building is one of the few that survived the 1906 quake?"

Kaia's history geek-o-meter lit up. She'd read everything she could get her hands on about the history of the Bay Area when she moved here. She'd been known to inundate her family with trivia so badly on the phone that they occasionally avoided her calls.

Too flustered with lust to explain how amazing it was to be on a date with someone tossing out San Francisco factoids, she simply said, "Awesome, right?"

Their eyes moved away from the view, clashing together. They gazed at one another, lips upturned, eyes locked. It would have been a hell of a moment if it hadn't been interrupted by Kaia's phone vibrating against her stomach.

Kaia instinctively shoved her hand into the pocket of her hoodie, retrieved the offending thing, and dropped it on the table beside her coffee. "Sorry about that."

"No worries." Lila touched her hand. "Happens to me all the time. Is it a work thing?"

Kaia glanced at the screen. "Veronica Turner" was displayed on the face. She involuntarily released a long, exasperated sigh.

Lila chuckled and released her hand. "Must be work."

"Yeah." Kaia hit the reject button and turned her attention back to her date. "Not important though."

Lila smiled and grasped Kaia's hand again. They went back to gazing into each other's eyes. "Okay, then."

"So, um, are you busy this weekend?"

Lila shook her head. "Nope. You?"

"No, I—"

The stupid phone vibrated again. This time it buzzed against the table with a low sound. With trepidation, Kaia glanced down to see the same name plastered across the screen.

Lila released her hand and sat back in the chair. "It's okay. Go ahead and answer it."

Kaia reluctantly picked up the phone and held it to her ear. "Hello?"

"Kaia. It's Veronica."

"Yeah. I know. What do you need?"

"Am I interrupting something?"

At that moment, the people-pleaser in Kaia didn't care if she sounded put out. Because she was, in fact, put out. Veronica's lack of boundaries, rude speech, and obnoxious calls were seriously getting on her nerves. "Actually, I'm on a date." She glanced at Lila who smiled sweetly at her.

"A date? With whom?"

Kaia swallowed down her irritation. She went for a tempered, but firm, tone. "What can I do for you?"

"Is this a serious girlfriend? Because Agnes said she didn't think you were in a relationship."

Kaia pulled the phone away from her ear and stared at it for a moment. Torn between being surprised that Agnes and Veronica had discussed her, and curious as to what was discussed and why, she decided to completely ignore the entire issue and deflect. "How can I help you?"

"We have permission for another interview with Jessica. I want to schedule it right away."

Kaia kept her voice as measured as possible. "I'd like to help, but I don't have Agnes's schedule with me. I can call you back when I get home, or you can call Agnes directly. I believe she's at home today."

"Well, I need to make sure you're free as well."

Kaia kept her voice professional rather than match the demanding tone of the woman on the line. "My schedule is very flexible. Whatever works for you and Agnes will work for me."

"Where are you right now?"

Kaia was stunned into silence. She glanced over at Lila, who sipped her coffee while casually gazing out the window. Why on earth did Veronica think she had the right to know everything about her and what she was doing? And why? That seemed to be the ultimate question. But there wasn't time to dig into that now. Kaia had a beautiful history geek waiting for her to get off the phone with the tigress and back to their date.

"I'll call you when I get home." Kaia pulled the phone away from her ear and smashed her finger on the end button.

"Sorry about that," she told Lila.

Lila turned back from the window. "It's okay. Where were we?"

Chapter Six

Kaia looked incredibly stunning. She sat across from Veronica at Agnes and Helen's kitchen table, a glass of wine cradled in her hands and a beautiful glow to her cheeks. She laughed and leaned her head back to expose a little divot at the base of her neck that Veronica desperately wanted to taste. Did everyone have that? Why had Veronica never noticed that before?

Helen emerged from the kitchen balancing a large platter in her hands. "I was super careful. I cleaned the kitchen before I made this." Helen set the platter in the center of the table. Carefully arranged slices of gourmet cheese sat surrounded by a ring of olives and anchored by odd-looking round things that might have wanted to be crackers but appeared to be more of a squished pile of seeds than any cracker Veronica had ever seen.

Helen threw her statement into the room casually. She didn't look at Kaia as she said it. But everyone knew it was aimed at her, including Veronica. She'd spent time on the Internet checking into Kaia's disorder. Apparently, even tiny amounts of flour or bread from cross contamination during food preparation could make a person with Celiac disease sick. The whole thing seemed like a major pain-in-the-ass, which she supposed explained why Kaia was so sensitive about it.

Kaia thanked Helen in an adorable, soft voice. Since no one else moved, she filled a small plate with an assortment of items and sat back with the plate on the table nestled between her forearms. She smiled and waved her hand around the table in a gentle gesture of invitation.

Veronica took the hint. She wanted to be the one to make Kaia feel more comfortable. She set down her glass of chardonnay to reach for one of the pairs of wooden tongs and used them to pull items onto the little ceramic plate that sat sadly empty in front of her for the last twenty minutes.

"What are these things?" She held up one of the round items posing as a cracker.

"They're gluten-free crackers." The answer came from Kaia instead of Helen. "They're my favorite. Thanks again, Helen."

"You don't have to thank me. It's no big deal." Helen dropped into her seat beside Veronica and smiled fondly at Kaia.

"It is a big deal," Kaia said. "Most people don't like to go to so much trouble." She stared down at her plate, mouth turned down at the corners.

"It's no trouble," Helen said.

"And people suck," Agnes added.

"I don't know why anyone wouldn't bend over backward for someone like you." The words left Veronica's mouth, as usual, without much consideration for how they might be perceived. So skilled at carefully choosing her words in court, once outside of that specific venue, her tongue was a loose cannon.

Instead of acknowledging Veronica's outburst, Agnes plunged forward with the business of the evening. "Let's talk questions. I want a solid set of questions for Jessica's next interview." Agnes pointed her finger toward Veronica. "And I want your help in getting her to answer them."

Veronica nodded, surprised at her own relaxed reaction to being commanded to do something. Somehow, it didn't raise her ire. The only explanation she had for that was the presence of the woman across from her.

"What do you think we should lead with, Kaia?" Veronica asked.

In mid-motion, carefully stacking a cracker with cheese, Kaia abandoned her task and folded her hands on the table. "Based on my research, I think we need to drill down on her legal documents. But I realize we need to slide into that. I suggest we start by asking about her marriage to Gregory."

"I agree," Agnes said. She made a note on a pad in front of her. "I planned to start with a few questions about her husband. What was the marriage like? What were the good times like? That kind of thing. Then I was going to get into when it all went bad."

"Wait. Back up," Veronica said. "What do you mean about her legal documents?" Out of the corner of her eye, Veronica caught movement from Helen, who hadn't said a word. But when she bent down and picked up little Pookie to snuggle in her arms, she brought the elephant into the room—Veronica's tied up money. "We already went through all that."

"There's a lot more to unpack there," Kaia said simply.

Veronica pinned Kaia with her gaze. Used to being the legal authority in the room, she treated everyone, even gorgeous techs who claimed to know something about the law, with extreme skepticism.

Agnes broke the moment. "So, we start with an overview of the marriage from the wedding on, since we already talked through dating and engagement."

"I'm guessing she already knows all about it." Veronica pointed her finger toward Kaia. In this case, though, Veronica was impressed. Of all the private investigators she'd hired over the years to help her with cases, Kaia seemed to best them all in her ability to uncover an incredible amount of information in a very short period of time.

Agnes chuckled. "She does. And she gave me a whole report. That's not the point. We want to hear it in Jessica's words."

"What if she lies?" Veronica nearly slapped her hand over her mouth. The spontaneous thought slipped out of her lips, and she couldn't take it back.

Ignoring the deeper implications, Agnes had an immediate answer. "Then we call her out on it. We're investigative reporters. That's what we do."

Veronica knew from the beginning she wasn't dealing with a pushover in Agnes. She needed the publicity for Jessica, and she needed someone who would give her a chance. That's why she'd called in the first place. There would be no molding Agnes to her will.

However, because Veronica's belief in Jessica's innocence was complete and total, she hadn't anticipated a snag like this. Jessica was bound to lie. It was practically a part of her DNA. It made her look guilty as hell, even though she wasn't. So what if she lied to Agnes and Kaia? Would that tank Veronica's entire plan?

Veronica schooled her features, tucking away her concerns in the depths of a great poker face. "Okay. I'll keep her from lying. Let's move on. What's next?"

"We'll move to the end," Agnes said. "We'll ask what their relationship was like in the weeks and days before Gregory was murdered."

"Disappeared," Veronica said.

"Technically, yes." Kaia laid her hands on the table in front of her as if presenting a gift. "No body has been found."

A warm tingling floated through Veronica's chest.

"But," Kaia continued, breaking the cozy feeling with that one, horrific word. "There was more than enough of his blood found soaked into the library rug and on the hardwood floor around it to safely assume he must be dead. No human can live with that much blood loss."

"That's what the prosecutor said, yes." Veronica pressed her lips together.

"Murdered or disappeared, the man is nowhere to be found, and Jessica never seemed all that upset about it," Agnes said.

Veronica was about to argue that Jessica didn't get emotional over living things, until her attention snagged on that damn dog snuggled into Helen's arms. Jessica would lay down her life for that thing. With that argument shot to hell, she turned to another one. "So she didn't like him very much. So what?"

"Some people call that motive," Agnes said.

"No, my dear. That is motive for divorce, not murder. And remember, the money is hers, not his."

"Actually, its no one's at the moment," Kaia said. "Except maybe Pookie's." She gestured to the tiny dog now fast asleep with her head tucked into Helen's elbow. "The only thing the money can be accessed for is her. The trustee is in charge of that."

"Okay. Let's get to it," Veronica said. "Tell me what you think you know about the financials."

Kaia took a breath so deep it was audible in the room. She rolled her shoulders back and lifted her head. "The paperwork is extremely clear and legally ironclad."

Veronica nodded, but stopped herself from opening her mouth. Of course she knew this. She was an attorney, and she'd seen the same paperwork. Her instinct to make it clear that she knew what the hell she was doing bubbled to the surface. But, in a moment completely uncharacteristic of herself, Veronica kept her mouth shut. She wanted to hear Kaia speak, and that desire overtook even her own ego.

Kaia's eyes flitted to Veronica. "I'm sure you know this. Do you really want me to start at the beginning?"

Veronica nodded. "Yes. I want to hear your perspective. You know, the layman's perspective." She cringed internally. Attempts to keep her attitude in check were failing. Experience told her that exposing her pride usually turned people against her. "Plus, I'm sure Helen wants to hear this."

Helen stroked Pookie's head and nodded.

"Okay, well, all of Jessica's money goes into a trust the moment Jessica becomes incapacitated."

"And what exactly does that entail?" Helen asked.

Kaia gazed at Helen with her head held far higher than usual. "Essentially, anything that makes her incapable of managing her own affairs. So, let's say she ends up on your operating table. The time she's unconscious would be time that all her money was in the trust, even if it was only for a few hours."

"Like the President. The Vice takes over if he—"

"Or she," Agnes said.

Helen grinned. "Yeah, or she, is under general anesthetic. The Vice President is in charge of the country during that time."

"Pretty much, yeah. And in Jessica's case it's not just for health reasons either. It could also be because she's kidnapped or held against her will."

"This is the part that includes jail," Agnes added.

"Yes," Kaia said. "While the document doesn't specifically mention jail—because I'm sure Jessica never planned to end up there—it does specifically identify a situation where she is being held in a place where she does not have free access to the outside world. This clearly includes imprisonment."

Veronica's head swum with pride. It filled her being despite being misplaced, as Kaia and she had no real connection. Yet, Veronica already thought of Kaia as being a part of her life. Her crush was real. So real.

"Why would someone make a document like this?" Agnes asked.

"There are a couple of reasons," Kaia said. "First, Jessica inherited a massive fortune. All that money goes to her niece upon her death. She is the child of her late brother. And Jessica and her sister-in-law—the mother of the girl—get along about as well as Democrats and Republicans. So the idea is to protect the money so the sister-in-law can't drain the accounts while she's out of commission."

"But why the extremes?" Helen asked. "Like the clause about being incapacitated. Does she have health problems where she would expect to be having a lot of surgeries or something?"

Veronica opened her mouth to speak, but clamped it shut again and turned to Kaia. Kaia paused and her eyes locked with Veronica for one, brief, intense moment. When Veronica nodded, Kaia spoke. "She was kidnapped twice as a kid. And her brother once. Held for ransom."

Helen's jaw dropped, and Agnes shook her head. "That would leave a lot of trauma."

Veronica waited to see if Kaia had anything else to add. Kaia leaned back in her seat and deflated her lungs, giving the clear signal that she was done.

"So, that's the scoop. Now how does it relate to the murder case?" Agnes asked.

"Wait," Helen said. "Where does Pookie come in?"

Veronica leaned forward, examining the pup in Helen's arms. The thing looked pretty harmless really, even if it was an uncontrollable creature with sharp teeth. "There is a single exception to the money being completely inaccessible. The trustee can get into the account and retrieve money needed for Pookie's care and maintenance."

"Oh." Helen's voice was quiet.

"Do you need some money?" Veronica asked.

"No," Helen replied quickly.

"Absolutely not," Agnes said. "We can take care of her."

"So," Veronica turned back to Kaia, "what's your take on all this legal stuff? What does it have to do with Gregory's disappearance?"

"Well," Kaia placed her hand on the table and traced the patterns in the wood grain, "I haven't fully figured that out yet. But I can see that it might make sense to have Jessica incapacitated but not dead."

"So they kill her husband and frame her?" Agnes asked.

Kaia shrugged. "It's certainly a possibility. It'd be easier than kidnapping a feisty woman like Jessica who's probably learned a lot about how not to get abducted."

"Exactly!" Veronica felt like a sailboat that just hit the wind. Kaia walked her right into the best possible defense for her client. She wanted to leap across the table and kiss her on the mouth.

****

Living in the city, Kaia knew the sensation of being followed. It was simply a part of life to have a proverbial eye on your back. Most of the time, a faster walker, a skateboarder, or a jerk riding an electric scooter on the sidewalk instead of in the bike lane like they were supposed to, moved in from behind. But even if they posed no threat—aside from the potential to end up on crutches from the stupid scooter—she could always sense them back there.

Now the click of heels attached to shapely legs gained on her as she made her way toward the parking garage one block away from Agnes and Helen's place. She pretended not to notice and continued at exactly the same speed. There was no point in going faster. Even in her Chucks, her short limbs were no match for the model-worthy attorney.

As she passed under a streetlamp there was a quick tug on the back of her sweatshirt. No longer able to ignore Veronica's presence, Kaia stopped and spun around. She looked up at the face glowing under the streetlamp that created an unwanted spike in awareness. Veronica's beauty bordered on terrifying.

"Can I help you?" Kaia congratulated herself on keeping her voice measured.

"Can I give you a ride home?"

"No thanks. I'm good." Kaia turned toward the intersection that separated her from the pedestrian entrance to the garage.

"What about dinner?" Veronica's question was accompanied by another tug, this time on Kaia's sleeve.

"What?" Kaia whirled around again.

"Dinner, with me, tomorrow night," Veronica said. "I'll cook it myself and it will be safe. We can eat at my house. What do you think?"

Kaia's eyes strained wide, she thought they must look like giant disks. Confusion warred with her desire to flee. As a result, she was stuck there to the sidewalk, unable to move. "Why?"

"Because I want to spend more time with you."

The bossy, straight woman with zero sense of compassion and serious swagger wanted to spend time with her? There was only one logical reply. "Why?"

Veronica smiled then. It wasn't the cocky grin she usually sported. This smile was almost timid, so completely out of place on Veronica's face it caused Kaia's confusion to override the better sense to run for her life.

Then it happened. Out of the clear blue sky—or in this case the dark city night—Veronica leaned down, placed her well-manicured hands on either side of Kaia's face and moved in for a kiss.

Kaia snapped herself out of the trance just in time. She yanked her head back and took a step away from Veronica, slipping out of her grasp. "What are you doing?"

Veronica stood there, hands hanging in mid-air, expression unreadable. "I want to kiss you."

Anger welled up in Kaia so fast it burst out of her. "Didn't you think you should ask me? You just take what you want? What the hell?"

Veronica blinked. Her hands fell to her sides. "I...I hadn't really thought about that."

"Do you make it a habit of kissing people without consent?

Because there are programs for people like you. And maybe you should enroll, girl." Kaia was propelled away from Veronica, her anger far outweighing the questions lingering in the back of her mind.

"No. No. Actually, I haven't...I...I'm sorry." In the harsh glow of the street light Veronica's face was crystal clear, especially now that Kaia had retreated into the darkness. Devastated, stricken, and on the verge of tears—it was all there to see.

Kaia's empathy drew her forward, one small step toward this woman who was clearly swimming in pain. But whatever demon haunting Veronica pulled the strings, and the woman fled into the dark night.

Chapter Seven

The Basset Hound Kaia walked had no desire to keep up with the Husky mix tugging at the end of the leash Heath held onto. "Come on, Tut, let's catch up to Heath and Mika. Don't you want to hang out with them?"

Completely uninterested, Tut continued to amble along. Kaia sighed. She'd waited three days until their weekly dog-walking gig with the local SPCA. Desperate to talk to Heath about her situation, she knew they'd have lots of alone time. But Tut and Mika didn't want to cooperate.

"I'm going to head to the dog park so he can run," Heath called over his shoulder.

An excruciating ten minutes later, Heath released Mika into the fenced-in park and collapsed onto a wooden bench. Kaia plopped down beside him and unhooked Tut's leash from his harness. The dog sank into a heap at her feet and let out a loud sigh before promptly falling asleep.

Heath stared at the purebred dog. "I can't for the life of me figure out why someone would surrender such a chill dog." He shook his head.

"People are stupid," Kaia said.

Heath chuckled. "Ain't that the truth?"

Kaia tapped his ribs with her elbow. "How's the new job, hot shot news anchor?"

"Our show doesn't count as news."

"Sure it does. You report on true things."

Heath grinned at her. "I report on murder. Just murder."

"And who doesn't love that? How's it going?"

"Good. I get imposter syndrome daily. But, you know, good."

Kaia touched his shoulder. "Well, I've been watching and you've been killing it—pun intended."

"Thanks. How goes the podcast business? You guys are getting ready for the new season, yeah?"

"Yeah. I just put the promos together."

Heath rubbed his hands as if in anticipation of an amazing steak dinner. "I can't wait to see what you and Agnes do with Jessica French."

"Huh. Well, it's going to be a major challenge."

"Yeah. That chick is eeeviiil."

Kaia peeked up at him from under her lashes. "It's not so much Jessica that's the problem. At least for me."

Heath cocked his head. "Oh yeah?"

Kaia had practiced this conversation in her head several times. She was desperate to get this all out. She'd chosen Heath as her confessor, and she was prepared. That is, until it was time to actually come out with it. Her brain seemed to head in every direction but the one she needed.

"It's, um, it's…the attorney…you know."

"You mean Veronica Turner?"

Kaia nodded.

"She's something else, that lady. I worked with her when Helen was accused of killing Jolie Green."

"What did you think of her?"

Heath stroked his chin with his thumb and forefinger. "She's competent, confident, courageous…girl is fierce. And she says what she means."

"And takes what she wants."

Heath dropped his hand and stared at her. "Did something happen with Veronica?"

Kaia nodded, but didn't speak.

Heath turned on the bench, angling his body toward hers. "Kaia. Tell me."

All her plans to sort through the complexities of her feelings about Veronica, from when she was deeply attracted to her in the club to the push and pull of their near kiss the other night, devolved into a single phrase. "It's fucked up."

Heath chuckled before cutting off the sound by slamming his palm over his lips. "I'm sorry. It's just that I so rarely hear you be blunt. What's fucked up about it?"

"She tried to kiss me." The end of the story somehow came out as the beginning. Not sure she could explain now that the beans were spilled, Kaia gazed at Heath, waiting for his response.

"Okay, and?"

"What do you mean, and? I mean, for starters, she's not a lesbian."

"Why would you say that?"

"Because her cousin, Malcolm, said so. I asked. In fact, she's only ever dated men."

"Apparently he's wrong."

The casual way he said that irked her. "I mean...what makes you say that?"

Keith rolled his eyes up toward the sky. "Are you not working for a bisexual woman who is married to a bisexual woman? I'm a little shocked that you're being so—"

She pointed her finger at him. "Don't say it. Okay, fine, so the chick is bi. But I honestly didn't see that coming."

"Maybe she didn't either."

Kaia absorbed that. It made the way it went down seem a little clearer. If Veronica was just now coming to terms with her attraction to women, it would explain a lot. It had to be confusing as hell to live thirty-some years and suddenly have to face your sexuality. Kaia could be empathetic to that.

That empathy took over her mind and seeped into her heart. The anger she'd felt at Veronica's assumption morphed. "Okay. Yeah. But she's so—"

"Intense?" Heath suggested.

"Yes."

A pause punctuated the space between them as Mika ran circles around the three Chihuahuas yipping at his knees. But Heath eventually broke it. "I noticed you didn't say anything about not being attracted to her."

Kaia's stomach clenched, but she remained motionless. The truth of Veronica's beauty seemed like an undeniable fact to her. That he would bring it up was pointless. Wasn't it? She decided to be evasive, even if she knew, deep down, it would never work. "I don't see how that's relevant."

"Ah Ha!" Heath slapped his knee, causing Tut to jolt awake. The dog gave them both side eye before tucking his head between his paws and falling back to sleep. "You do find her attractive!"

"Again. Not at all relevant."

Heath laughed. Kaia seethed. But she couldn't for one second lie.

****

"Why the hell do you want to know about my marriage? What business is it of yours?" Jessica's resting bitch face had morphed to full-fledged nightmare face.

Veronica neared her limit with the petulant blonde. Despite their long conversation about the value of this podcast to her case and the importance of sounding good to the audience, Jessica just couldn't stop herself from being unbelievably difficult.

Agnes took in a slow, deep breath before she spoke again. "I want to tell your story from beginning to end. You told us how you and Gregory met and how you quickly fell in love. We want to know what's next. Tell us about your marriage. It lasted for three years, yes?"

Jessica turned her head to stare at the peeling cream paint on the wall and said nothing.

"Damn it!" Frustration flooded Veronica. She pulled every string she had to help this woman. Over and over again, Jessica's pain-in-the-ass personality cut it all up like a pair of sharp scissors slicing through her efforts.

Even the patient Agnes was over this woman. She threw her hands in the air. "I can't."

There was nothing to be done now. They'd spent the last twenty minutes trying to get Jessica to give them something—anything. She'd oscillated between the silent treatment to snarky outbursts and back again. If Agnes gave up now, Veronica couldn't blame her. But she would also be in deep shit in terms of what to do to help Jessica.

Kaia's voice sliced through the tension. "Hold up, everyone." Every eye in the room swiveled to Kaia. She took a deep breath and continued. "I think we're losing sight of the goal here."

Jessica cocked her head, a motion Veronica was certain she'd never seen. The woman looked a little like a Golden

Retriever wondering if Kaia was going to throw her a tennis ball.

"Our goal here is to show the world that Jessica is innocent," Kaia said.

Agnes opened her mouth, her objection practically visible in the air. There was no way Agnes would cop to that. She had always been clear that her podcast was impartial, about the truth, and nothing else.

But Kaia placed a hand over Agnes' wrist, stopping her protest. "So, what's the best way to do that? What do you think, Jessica?"

Never, ever, had it occurred to Veronica to ask Jessica what she wanted to convey. She had always viewed the woman as an entity to be managed and controlled. But what did it hurt? It's not like any of this was live. Kaia could edit to her heart's desire. And why not let Jessica have what she really wanted—some control over her own life?

Jessica squared her shoulders and concentrated only on Kaia. If she could set up an invisible shield blocking Agnes and Veronica out, she probably would. "I want people to know I didn't kill Gregory. I want them to know that Gregory was...he was...kind of a dick to me." Jessica's eyes flitted to the side as she spoke this difficult truth.

Veronica's stomach tightened. Despite her sudden intense internal dedication to getting Jessica acquitted, she sat back in her chair and made a promise to herself not to say a word until Kaia was done.

Kaia leaned forward, her body open, her eyes kind. "I hear you. What did he do, Jessica?"

Jessica's throat visibly moved. Her eyes glistened as she blinked repeatedly. "He was a dick."

"Did he say asshole things?" Kaia's voice, quiet but firm, commanded the deep silence in the room while simultaneously demanding an answer from the woman who was at the center of her focus.

Jessica nodded. "All the time."

"That is so hard. It makes you feel like shit."

Jessica nodded again.

"What else?"

So quickly it was barely discernable, Jessica brushed

over her cheek with her fist before setting in on the table again. "Nothing else. Just words."

"Words can cut as deeply as a knife," Kaia said.

Jessica stared at Kaia, her eyes glued to the woman.

"I bet he wasn't the first one to hurt you with words," Kaia said.

Veronica could barely believe what she was witnessing. Jessica, entranced by the shy sound tech, allowed a tear to roll down her face, dripping off her chin and dropping onto the table. In the softest voice she had surely ever used, the woman replied. "No. My dad. Ex-boyfriends. Supposed friends. Lots of people."

The room nearly vibrated with intensity as Kaia reached her hand across the table and placed it over Jessica's. "I understand."

Veronica's mind shifted suddenly from her client to Kaia. Did she understand? What had she been through in her short life? How could Veronica help?

"I was planning to get a divorce," Jessica said.

Agnes spoke up then. "Did you tell anyone?"

Jessica shook her head. "I literally had plans to call my lawyer the day after I found the blood. I was tired. I'd been at a fundraising gala, and I just wanted to pull off my heels and go to bed. I planned to call Tom in the morning and tell him to fix this whole mess for me. I didn't expect Gregory to be home." Jessica pressed her palm against her forehead for a moment before looking back up at Kaia. "I figured he was at one of his girlfriend's houses. I wasn't upset about it. Not at that point. I just wanted some peace. But I walked past the library and something made me pause. I don't know what. Something. Anyway, I peeked in and saw the blood."

In the telling of this story in the past Jessica was always so straight forward—short, terse answers. Now she spoke with emotion and detail, leaving Veronica completely riveted. Literally biting her tongue, she waited for Kaia's next move.

"People must have seen you at the fundraiser," Kaia said.

Jessica straightened up. A loud sniff signaled the change in her demeanor. "Veronica said there were fourteen people willing to go on record that I was there. Doesn't matter though. I spent two hours at home getting ready. That's when the police say I killed him." A tiny hiccup escaped her throat. "But he wasn't even in the house then. At least, I don't think so. I can't prove it. That's the problem, right?"

Kaia flashed Jessica a smile so sweet and blinding Veronica thought she might melt. "We'll figure it out."

Chapter Eight

Kaia jerked with surprise as Agnes shoved her overflowing folder across the table. "I'm handing it all over."

"Wait. What?"

Agnes's expression was a combination of innocence and confidence. "Something came up."

Kaia waited, certain there was more to this than that ridiculously simple statement.

"Here's the thing." Agnes plunked her elbows on the table and leaned toward Kaia. "Some things are happening with the adoption. I need to be ready to travel on a moment's notice. Helen is a surgeon. It's a little harder for her to be flexible."

"Okay." None of this was new to Kaia. She understood that Agnes was the spouse with the malleable schedule, and that Agnes planned to stay home with the child when she came. Kaia knew the score when she took the job. She'd been told she would have more and more responsibilities to shoulder. She'd been warned that she might have to finish projects on her own. And she was prepared for all of it—until they'd taken on the Jessica French story.

"And rather than have a podcast with a bunch of holes in it because I'm focused elsewhere, if you take over now, it will be much smoother." Agnes leaned back in her chair. "Besides, I can't stand that woman. And you're so good with her."

"Jessica?" Kaia asked.

Agnes laughed. "Yes, I mean Jessica." Amusement flashed in her eyes. "Who did you think I meant?"

As far as Kaia was concerned, there were two difficult women in this gig. Her gaze stayed glued to the folder as she deflected. "But, um, are you sure I'm ready for this? I mean, I don't want to screw up your podcast. It's your baby."

"Kind of. Though with a real baby on the way, I'm a lot

less anal about it. Kaia," Agnes placed her hand on Kaia's wrist and left it there until Kaia shifted her gaze to look her in the eye, "I have complete faith in you on this. Besides, Heath said he's here to help, anytime."

Kaia bit her lip and swallowed hard. Agnes was putting an incredible amount of faith in her and she needed to come clean about her issues. "I'm not so sure I can work with Veronica."

A crease formed between Agnes's brows. "Why not?"

Kaia toyed with the idea of telling Agnes about how Veronica had tried to kiss her. But the confused and terrified look on Veronica's face in that moment when Kaia called her out haunted her. This woman—despite all her bluster—was in trouble. Should Kaia throw that into Agnes's hands right now, in the middle of everything? When Agnes had enough anxieties piling up—new baby, a newbie tech taking over her show, a wife with an intense job—wasn't it too much already? Kaia couldn't burden her with the vulnerable face she had gotten a glimpse of when Veronica lowered her mask in the dark city night.

"It's nothing." Kaia threw her hand across the space between them. "She's just a little much, you know?"

Agnes laughed. "Yeah. I know. But she's good people. I have complete confidence in you to keep her calm and keep Jessica talking."

Kaia hoped to hell she deserved that confidence.

****

Veronica's loving parents had nearly spoiled her, with one exception. They taught her to fight for what's right. The fierceness with which they instilled that value, and the depth of Veronica's personal commitment to it had led her to many great things, her career among them.

Her personal life didn't go unaffected either. She knew her white skin afforded her privileges the rest of her family never received, and it made her a loud and determined ally.

But the total failure of her life's guiding principle had

been intimate relationships. Somehow her parents' beloved flag of justice had been turned upside down when it came to the men in her life. Instead of fighting for herself, she fought to keep them, even when they were nothing but toxic.

Her worst failure—which ended in the humiliating involvement of her family—had led her mother to whisper between her tears, "You fight for everyone but yourself."

But Veronica had turned over that leaf. She'd made a vow to herself that she would never again be with the wrong person, even if that meant being with no one at all.

But then Kaia had shown up. Veronica wanted to explore all the things she'd been wondering about with Kaia—only Kaia. She was certain that the lovely, shy woman was not the wrong sort—the kind of person who would stomp on her and her heart.

But she'd made an error already. She moved too fast. Her confusion created the awkward moment on the side-walk. She understood that now. Days of analysis left her with three basic truths: one, she was definitely into women—specifically Kaia—and there was no point in fighting that. Two, she'd made an unwanted move, making her no better than a skeezy office perv, and she had to make up for that. And, three, she really, really wanted to try again, minus the creepy part.

Forging a plan relaxed Veronica, as it always did. Left to her own devices, Veronica was impulsive and did stupid things, like trying to kiss Kaia under a streetlamp. That's why she battled her impulses with careful planning. Every genius move she made in the courtroom was meticulously mapped out. Though she made it look like an incredible improv.

So she did the same thing with her plan to get Kaia to not see her as a she-devil. She laid it all out in her head, thinking through each interaction they'd had so far and how she needed to change the dynamic between them in the future. And there would be chances. Now that Kaia was taking over the entire podcast season, Veronica would get much more time with her.

The excitement over that prospect plummeted, landing hard at the bottom of her feet as she stared at her email. The

Corrections Department denied their next scheduled podcast visit because they were doing some sort of security drill that day. She would have to make a new request.

Veronica slammed her hand on her desk and by a grave miscalculation hit the edge of the stapler. Ribbons of pain shot up her arm that caused her to curse. The physical pain echoed her internal frustration. It was never a quick process to request a date for a media visit with a prisoner, and now she would have to wait to see Kaia.

Not to mention that her plan to get Jessica out of prison meant moving quickly. If everything went as she hoped she could have public opinion fully swayed to Jessica's innocence before the jury was even picked. But the Corrections Department just threw her carefully laid plans out the window.

Veronica realized she had to break the bad news. She wouldn't wait to make the dreaded call. She grasped the phone in her still-throbbing hand and dialed.

"Kaia here."

"Hi, Kaia. It's Veronica." Her voice spewed sugar and spice and everything nice.

"Um…what can I do for you?" The hesitancy in Kaia's tone reflected the errors of Veronica's past. She knew it would require face time to fix it.

"Our appointment with Jessica for tomorrow got canceled," Veronica said.

Kaia blew out a breath that struck the phone just right and echoed back at Veronica. It sounded like relief, but Veronica hated to think of it that way. She didn't want Kaia to be happy about delaying time with her. But that was inevitably what she felt. Because Veronica had really, really screwed up.

"Okay. Just let me know when the next date is and I'll be there," Kaia said.

"So, since you're free tomorrow, do you want to go out with me instead?" The words flew out of her mouth, but she didn't care. Now that she had Kaia on the phone, she was desperate to get her to meet in person. Maybe if she had the chance, she could find a way to turn this upside down and get Kaia to see her in a new light.

"Um... what do you mean?" Kaia asked, her voice hesitant.

Veronica pushed every bit of cheer she could into her words, her voice jolting up at the end of the sentence like a balloon floating into the air. "I mean go out. Me and you."

"Like, to talk about the case?"

Veronica sucked in a deep breath. She could be deceptive here. She knew from talking to Agnes that Kaia was nervous about taking over the podcast. She could totally use that to manipulate her into meeting up. But that would make her no better than Lane. And she was way better than Lane.

"No. I just wanted to see you."

"Like a date?"

Veronica's heartbeat drummed in her ears. Was she about to skip like three steps on her plan in one phone call? "Yes. Exactly like that."

"I'm sorry, Veronica. I don't think that's a good idea. Call me when you get the next date to see Jessica." Kaia hung up.

Veronica pressed her hands to her eyes for a long moment before sitting up. She shook off the failure and thought through her plan again, searching for the next step.

****

A few years back Kaia had taken a self-care seminar. The speaker encouraged everyone to select one of the self-care techniques she'd projected onto the screen behind her and stick to it. Kaia had selected the "day off." And she'd stuck to it.

One day of each week she didn't do any work. She didn't deal with the drudgery of life like bills and paperwork. She didn't stand in line at the bank. She didn't wade through emotionally difficult situations during awkward phone calls.

On that one day a week, she spent the day doing something she wanted to do. That day was Sunday, and on this Sunday Kaia was preparing to head to book club. They met once a month, and she loved it. Armed with a bottle of wine and the latest women's fiction selection under her arm, she was headed for the door when her phone rang.

Rule number one was to turn off the phone. But she'd forgotten. Two and half years into her routine, and she'd forgotten to turn off the phone. She reached for it and answered out of sheer curiosity. Her entire family, and every one of her friends knew it was her day off. They only called if there was an emergency or they needed directions to meet her somewhere for a day at the beach or a museum visit.

Assuming a book club member was calling, she hit speaker and held the phone in one hand while opening the door with the other. "Yeah?"

"Kaia?"

Kaia's stomach dropped to her feet. That voice was the sign that she'd just made a massive mistake. "Veronica."

"Listen, I know you said you were busy every Sunday for the rest of your life."

Kaia was surprised Veronica remembered her statement last week about that, but she took advantage of it. "That's right. I am. In fact, I'm headed out the door—"

"We got a last minute appointment with Jessica, and I think we should take it."

Kaia stopped in the doorway, backed up into her foyer, and let the door fall shut. They'd been told they'd have to wait between two and four weeks for their next meeting with Jessica. That would seriously push back her schedule for the podcast. A sooner date was a good thing.

Kaia dropped the book and wine on her kitchen counter and grabbed the notepad she kept on a magnet stuck to the fridge. She fished a pen out of the junk drawer, slammed it shut with her hip and leaned over the counter, her hands at the ready. "Okay. When?"

"Tomorrow morning. 9 a.m."

Kaia scribbled that down, not that she would forget. She glanced at her oven. They had thirteen hours to prepare. Damn.

As if Veronica had read her mind, she said, "We need to talk about it ahead of time."

Kaia wished she could argue, but this was Jessica. Everything needed to be carefully thought out or it could go off the rails in a matter of minutes. With Agnes out of the picture it was all up to her.

"Okay. Okay." Kaia tried to find an escape from the inevitable, but there was no way out. She couldn't plan this in the morning. She needed to talk it out with Veronica, then spend a few more hours preparing herself. This had to be done tonight. "Where can I meet you?"

"You hungry?"

Kaia rolled her eyes. She should have expected Veronica would try to turn this into a dinner date. "No. I ate already."

"Well, that's gonna be hard to explain to my mom and my aunts, but okay. I'll text you the address." With no further explanation, Veronica hung up.

Chapter Nine

Veronica possessed enough empathy to understand that walking into a Turner family gathering had to be an overwhelming experience. Her father's four brothers plus their wives and combined eleven children and six grandkids were all there, gathered in the garden behind the house her beloved grandparents had owned in the Fillmore until their deaths.

Uncle Chester and his wife Denise lived in the brownstone now and hosted the monthly gathering. Not attending was unacceptable. Only being confined to a hospital bed was a viable excuse, and even then, the whole clan was likely to show up and overwhelm the nursing staff.

Veronica loved her giant, intensely close family. But she felt a tinge of regret as she watched the tiny podcast producer swarmed by her aunts with plates of food and nearly inundated with requests to get her a drink from her male cousins before she'd even made it all the way through the gate.

Kaia had been running hard from Veronica since they met, how much worse would this make it?

Veronica pushed her way through her overeager family to extract Kaia from the fray. The hand she placed on Kaia's elbow to escort her into the garden burned. "Sorry about them. They get really excited about new people."

"Um. It's okay. They seem really nice."

"They are. Too, nice." Veronica shooed her niece, Janelle, out of a seat near the end of one of the long tables and deposited Kaia there, slipping onto the bench beside her.

Almost as soon as her butt hit the wooden bench, a plate piled with brisket, cornbread, greens, and potato salad was slipped in front of Kaia by Aunt Lisa, followed by a beer from her cousin Ryan.

Malcolm shooed Ryan away and took over his spot on

the opposite side of Kaia from Veronica. "Hey, Kaia."

Kaia seemed to relish the friendly face, even if they were only recently acquainted. According to Malcolm, he'd spoken to Kaia several times in the last couple of weeks. Though Veronica had been unable to get him to tell her why or about what. The jerk had held that information just out of her reach the way he used to hold her favorite stuffed animals above her head when she was a kid.

Malcolm's change in position caused all the family dogs to shift from lying where he'd been at the other table to taking up residence around him in his new seat. It was always like that. It didn't matter whose dog it was, if Malcolm was around, they gravitated to him.

Kaia smiled at the pack of mismatched mutts settling around them. "I see why you became a dog trainer."

"Couldn't do much with Pookie, though," he said, referring to Jessica's tiny terror. "I guess she pooped on the carpet again at Agnes and Helen's place." He turned to look at Veronica. "You better get Jessica out of jail so she can take that monster back."

Veronica took a sip of her wine and glared at him. "Guess you better train the thing better."

Malcolm laughed. "Dog hater."

Kaia's head swiveled toward her, eyes wary. "You hate dogs?"

Veronica pierced Malcolm with her best angry, laser gaze. He didn't flinch. He'd never been the least bit bothered by her withering gaze. None of her cousins were. She could fell whole rooms of hardened attorneys with her glare, but it had no effect whatsoever on her family. "No. I mean, I'm just—"

"Afraid of them. She's actually afraid of them," Jon said from her right.

Veronica sighed. Bringing Kaia here was a terrible idea.

But it got worse. "It's because she got bit as a kid," her mother said and slipped into another seat near Kaia. She leaned her chin on her hand and stared openly at the poor woman.

And this—this was Veronica's fault. She'd confided in her mother that she was attracted to Kaia. Her mother had taken it well—too well. She'd managed to tell most of the family by the time Kaia drove the mile and half to the house.

"Oh." Kaia's face softened. "That sucks."

"It did. But I don't hate dogs."

Malcolm scoffed.

"I'm sure I'll like yours when you get it." Veronica wasn't sure her voice had ever sounded so desperate. She wanted to run into the house and lock herself in the pink and yellow bathroom where she'd first learned how to use a tampon.

"Ah, yes. The dog." Malcolm smiled knowingly. "I get her next."

"What are you talking about?" Veronica asked.

Malcolm smirked at her. "That's what Kaia and I have been arranging. The dog is with a trainer who specializes in gluten detection now. When she's mastered that, I'm going to take her to refine her behavior skills so she can pass the public access test."

Instead of yelling at Malcolm for keeping this secret from her like she wanted to, Veronica schooled her features and tried to keep her focus on the subject at hand. "What does that mean?"

"I'll teach her how to behave in restaurants and grocery stores so she can work for Kaia and keep her safe."

Kaia smiled, but Malcolm's mention of the dog's training led to an uncomfortable conversation about the food that had been piled in front of Kaia. As quickly as it was placed on the table the heaping plate and beer were whisked away. A hard cider and bag of gluten free chips someone found in the house took their place.

The pink in Kaia's cheeks betrayed her embarrassment over her condition. It was plain as day to Veronica. She tried to fight the urge, but the quality that made her a good lawyer was irrepressible. "Why does it embarrass you? The Celiac disease?"

Sometimes her family acted as a filter to her direct questions, and she half expected that now. But they didn't. They seemed just as interested in the answer. The air in the garden was laden with curiosity as they waited.

Kaia took a few deep breaths. She took a long sip of cider then folded her hands on top of the table. "It's...people don't understand. And it was worse before. I was in high school and already...different. Even before I came out, everyone knew I was queer." Her eyes bounced around the table. But the Turner family, accepting and riveted by her story, remained silent. In fact, this may have been the quietest the garden had ever been.

"And then, suddenly, I had to eat special food. It was just one more thing. We'd go to get pizza, and I sat there drinking cola. We had birthday cake...I don't know, it sounds dumb. But it's embarrassing. And people always want to talk about it and... sometimes I just want to be normal and eat a freaking piece of cake and not talk about it. But just a tiny bit makes me really sick."

Veronica's mother may be one of the most compassionate people on earth. It was a big joke among the family that Veronica seemed to be her opposite. So she could have almost predicted that her mother would reach across the old scarred picnic table and touch Kaia's hand. "Well, you're safe here to be exactly who you are."

As if to punctuate the point, Tara popped her head up from the other side of the table and knelt on the bench so she could be seen above the heads of the adults surrounding her. Her thin frame made her look more like eight than twelve. "I'm a girl," she told Kaia. "Even though I wasn't born that way."

Veronica's aunt Trish patted her shoulder and smiled. "Yes, you are, baby girl."

Veronica studied Kaia's expression. Her family had made her last boyfriend squirm. But Kaia's usually tight shoulders relaxed further with each word spoken. Somewhere between her mother's soft hand and Tara's endearing announcement, the expression on Kaia's face morphed from overwhelmed and embarrassed to happy. She practically glowed, and Veronica thought her heart might never be the same.

****

Veronica had taken the bus to her aunt and uncle's house. That was a massive surprise to Kaia. Even as Veronica rode in the passenger seat of her truck, she couldn't imagine the fashionable lawyer riding the bus.

"Turn here, you can park in the garage. I get an extra spot I never use."

Kaia hooked into a tight space that led to a dark underground garage. Her truck cleared the ceiling by a couple spare inches. Veronica handed her a white card to wave in front of the reader. A creaky, metal gate raised and allowed them entry.

After an excruciating parking experience, Kaia left her truck wedged between a tiny electric car and a giant concrete post. She dutifully followed Veronica to an elevator.

Veronica hit a button and pivoted on her high heels. "Sorry we didn't get much done there. My family is kinda—"

"Awesome. Your family is awesome." There was no reason not to let Veronica know that she'd had one of the best evenings in a long time with her amazing relatives. It was the truth, and Kaia was still riding on a bit of a high from the invitation she'd gotten to the next family gathering.

Veronica smoothed down the hem of her dress, the most formal clothing of anyone at the barbeque, and smiled. "Yes. I'm very lucky."

"Was it hard? I mean, with people being dicks. I think a white kid adopted by Black parents is still less common than the other way around. I imagine there were problems. Things being what they are."

"Yes. It was hard on them." Veronica gazed into her eyes, suddenly intensely serious. "Not many people are brave enough to ask about that."

The elevator door opened and Kaia couldn't help but cock her head in curiosity. She wondered if people didn't ask because they didn't want to broach the subject or because of Veronica herself. Until this evening, Kaia had seen her as unapproachable. But that had all changed when she'd watched Veronica's mom wipe mustard off her chin and her cousin, Bobby, pick her up and pretend he was going to toss her into the Koi pond.

Kaia followed Veronica into the elevator, still waiting for more. She thought she might have to ask, prompting the information she wanted, but once they were on their way up, Veronica continued her story. "They had the police called on them several times. People thought I'd been kidnapped. I don't remember most of the instances. Just a couple. Once when I was six and again when I was eight. Anyway, the world is messed up. But I'm blessed."

Veronica plunged out of the elevator into a long, dimly lit hallway. Kaia trailed as she silently padded over the thin, patterned carpet to a door near the end. Veronica used her key, swung open the door, and led the way into the apartment.

Kaia's expectations were all dashed in an instant. There had been no doubt in her mind that Veronica lived in some high-end penthouse. She was successful and well-dressed and should have been perfectly capable of affording at least a two- bedroom apartment in the city.

The cramped studio with a single window was a definite shock. The door practically hit the kitchen sink, which featured a stained, old faucet. The tiny kitchen led to a square space packed with a loveseat, bed, and glass coffee table. It was the pad of a newly graduated intern, not a successful lawyer.

Speechless, she let Veronica get her settled on the loveseat with a glass of wine before sitting beside her and demanding words. "I know what you're thinking."

"You do?" Kaia asked.

"Why do I live like this?"

Too surprised to use her natural filter, Kaia blurted, "Yeah, why?"

Veronica laughed, but the sound was off, as if there was no real mirth behind it. "You really wanna hear the story?"

What an odd question. Of course she wanted to hear the story. What person wouldn't? Kaia nodded.

Veronica sat back against the fluffy cushion of the brown and grey loveseat and swirled the wine in her glass. "I was with a man for a few years. My boyfriend— fiancé— his name was Lane. He was...he's a lawyer, too. At my old firm. In fact, I have this whole story about why I left the firm, but he definitely had something to do with it."

Kaia had no clue where this was going. But Veronica's pain in telling the story vibrated across the small space between them.

Veronica took a tender sip of wine and continued. "I don't know what it was about him. Or me at that time. I've always been...I've always been pretty bold."

Kaia smiled. "Good word for it."

"I mean, I grew up with all these amazing male cousins who taught me not to take any shit from anyone. And I usually don't. But Lane...there was something about him—about us—that was different. I let him..." She sucked in a deep breath and expelled it with an audible whoosh. "He hit me."

Kaia nearly fell off the couch. It wasn't the first time a person had confessed something like this to her. As heartbreaking and horrible as it was, it rarely elicited the level of shock Veronica's confession did.

She was trying desperately to wrap her mind around a woman like Veronica being in an abusive relationship. It wasn't that anyone in the world wasn't susceptible to abuse. Kaia cognitively knew that. It was just that Veronica was so hardened, so clearly of her own mind. It was so difficult to imagine her in a relationship at all, let alone an abusive one.

This revelation was challenging everything. Veronica was challenging everything.

"Anyway, if you do come to another family Sunday, don't say anything. None of my male cousins or uncles know. They'd... well, let's just say I'd end up defending them in court." Veronica gave her a lopsided smile and then clasped her hands together. "The last straw was when he hit my mom. That's when I left. I had to leave everything behind, including the money in our joint bank account. I had to start from scratch with loans to start my firm. Everything I've made in the last few years is sunk into that." She took a deep breath and plastered on a smile. "Shall we talk about Jessica? Do you need to take notes?"

"I don't...I mean, why didn't you tell anyone in your family? Why didn't your mom?" Kaia cringed. She hadn't meant to make Veronica even more uncomfortable. But she'd met the Turner family, and something just wasn't adding up.

Veronica twisted her fingers in her lap. "I begged my mom. I'm her weakness. I promised to leave him and never look back if she would keep my secret." Veronica's big eyes met Kaia's. "Can we not talk about this anymore?"

Kaia nodded and plunged into work. It left her no time to contemplate her changing view of Veronica. She pushed aside her confusion and compassion and committed to focusing on Jessica and her fight for freedom.

Three hours later, Veronica passed out on the couch, her head resting against a blue throw pillow, the cream-colored fringes ringing it lying over her forehead, teasing the tops of her closed eyelids. Not too exhausted to feel horribly guilty about taking Veronica's bed, Kaia swung her feet up on the hard mattress and turned on her side, facing the little couch that sat just out of arm's length.

With just the dim glow of the stove light illuminating the single room, Veronica's features reflected a quiet peace she never expressed while conscious. Kaia couldn't look away.

Everything was on its head. Kaia felt a million miles away from where she'd been just hours ago. She'd truly seen Veronica for the first time, and now her eyes, her heart, and her soul were drawn to the woman lying across the cramped room from her.

Chapter Ten

Veronica knew exactly what happened the night before. She'd known it as she'd closed her eyes that night, and she'd known it when she opened them this morning. Somewhere between her confession about Lane and the laughter they'd shared over a video from Agnes of Pookie attempting to keep the other dogs off the massive dog bed in their living room, she'd realized this wasn't just a crush.

Veronica couldn't bare her soul to a crush. She wouldn't let down her guard for someone she merely felt lust for. She hadn't ever laughed so freely with someone she merely found attractive. No, the truth was, she was completely in love with Kaia.

She also knew that unrequited love was a bitch. She wouldn't be able to change the situation. She couldn't make this woman love her in return. She knew that. She'd already screwed that up, and there was no taking it back.

So sitting beside Kaia in her car as they drove to the prison that morning was awkward, to say the least. Kaia's shoulders were tense, her lips pressed together, her hands closed into tight fists. She vibrated with tension that made Veronica wonder if she'd read her mind the night before, or worse, if the couple of glasses of wine Veronica drank had loosened her tongue.

She scoured her brain for something she may have done or said that wasn't at the top of her mind this morning. But she couldn't remember anything. There were only so many ways to find out how someone felt, especially someone like Kaia. Sharing emotions didn't seem to be big on Kaia's to-do list. Not that it was ever on Veronica's either—at least not until she'd fallen head over heels for a shy podcaster.

Perhaps small talk was the best place to start. "Are you ready for this?"

Kaia glanced over at her. "No." She laughed, the sound tinged with nervousness. "I'm not at all ready to do this without Agnes. To tell you the truth, I'm terrified I'll screw it up."

"But I thought you'd done interviews alone before? Something about a killer's mom? So, this isn't entirely new, right?"

Kaia shook her head, tendrils of short brown hair flying around her ears. "But somehow it's different in my mind. I don't know if I can fully explain it. But this entire podcast is on me now, and, frankly, I'm scared."

Veronica's mouth dropped, shocked by Kaia's easy admittance of her fear. That the reserved woman opened herself up like that had her reeling. The little spot in her heart that was now reserved just for Kaia throbbed.

It took Veronica a moment to compose herself, but when she did, she found the perfect thing to say. "You are one hundred percent ready for this, you just don't know it. You're more prepared than Agnes ever was for Jessica, and you're better with her than I am."

Veronica stopped at a light and took the opportunity to glance over at her passenger. Kaia shrugged and smiled, the casual body language so strange and confusing that Veronica quickly turned back to the road in front of her.

"The truth is..." Kaia released a heavy breath that traveled across the small space to hit Veronica lightly on the neck, causing the outbreak of a riot in her stomach. "I went to school for the tech side of this. And I feel confident about my ability to do that. But talking, that's not my thing."

"Really?" Veronica couldn't filter herself now. The cheerleader she wanted to be for Kaia seeped through. "Because you bested us all when it came to talking to Jessica the last time we did this."

"Yeah. But that was different."

Veronica scrunched up her nose. "How so?"

"I mean. I was just talking to her."

"Okay. And why is today different?"

"Because...oh shit." Kaia went quiet.

Veronica practically jumped out her skin. She silently begged Kaia to tell her what she was thinking. But the silence went on too long. As Veronica pulled the car into the lot behind the jail, she felt the overwhelming urge to push

Kaia out of her comfort zone and force her to speak, to show more of herself to Veronica—everything if possible. "Why is it different?"

"It isn't," Kaia said softly.

Veronica swung the car into a spot in the center of the lot. As soon as she'd slammed the gearshift into park she twisted her torso so she could face Kaia. "What do you mean?"

Kaia matched her, turning so they were face-to-face in the tiny, stuffy space of the car. Kaia pierced Veronica with her deep, brown eyes. "I wasn't thinking about the recording last time. I was just thinking about what I thought would speak to Jessica, you know? She seemed like she was in pain and I wanted to help her."

Kaia had a skill Veronica would never have—the ability to turn empathy into real, meaningful conversation. For Veronica, empathy was a tool she used against a jury to make a winning case. But for Kaia it was genuine, real, and came naturally to her. Veronica had never appreciated that trait until now. Strength in the face of a challenge had always been equated with hard and cold in her mind. But now she was fully lost in admiration for the courage it took to open up and show your heart the way Kaia did.

"I know this sounds stupid, but I forgot we were recording."

"So now that you remembered, how do you feel?" Veronica asked.

"Now I'm acutely aware that we're recording and I can't edit out my voice, because Agnes isn't here to provide the other interviewer voice. Does that make sense?" Kaia tilted her head in the most adorable way.

Veronica nodded, but words escaped her—a rare event seemingly reserved only for Kaia. Instinctively, she spoke with a touch and reached out to place her hand over Kaia's. The move must have come from her mother, a common gesture used to provide comfort and warmth. Without her knowledge, that simple but important act must have seeped its way into Veronica's repertoire.

Their two hands rested on top of the car's center console. One small, deeply tanned, and with work-worn fingers.

On top of it lay long, impossibly pale fingers, decorated with talons so frequently manicured they barely looked real anymore, at least in comparison to those beneath.

They both stared at the pile of fingers. The buzzing warmth that traveled up Veronica's arm was unmistakable. So was the pain in her chest at the knowledge that nothing she could ever do would make what she felt echo in the heart of the woman beside her.

The ache forced Veronica to move. Her hand flitted to her seatbelt where she worked quickly to get free so she could shove the door open and jump out of the car.

Kaia moved at a slower pace. When they met on the sidewalk in front of the jail, Veronica meant to hustle into the building, but Kaia pressed a hand to her elbow. "Wait."

That one little word forced Veronica to meet Kaia's gaze.

Kaia's deep brown eyes were like pools of open truth. Veronica wanted to drown in them. Kaia's lips opened and she said just two words, "Thank you." But to Veronica she might as well have said goodbye.

****

Somewhere between the electric touch in Veronica's car and being seated in the little interview room in the jail, Kaia gave herself a pep talk. She convinced herself she could, in fact, get what she needed for the podcast in the limited forty-five-minute window they'd been granted.

She took a deep breath and shot off her first question to the woman across from her. "Jessica, last time we spoke, you mentioned that you were planning to divorce Gregory just before he went missing. Can you tell me more about that?"

Jessica twisted her fingers, lacing them into odd shapes. Her gaze remained fixed on those acrobatic digits. Her breath echoed through the room, deep and ragged. This was not the cold, composed woman Kaia had met during their first interview.

Kaia knew she needed to back up and take care of Jessica's needs first and leaned over the table. She laid one hand over Jessica's. Beneath her palm, all movement stopped. Jessica's gaze shot up to meet hers.

Kaia smiled sweetly. "I saw Pookie yesterday."

Jessica's voice, ragged, strained, pushed out from dry, cracked lips. "You did? How is she?"

"She's good. I mean, I know she misses her mama, but she's happy. She gets along really well with the other two dogs she's living with. She has a big fluffy bed and gets lots of treats."

The corners of Jessica's mouth turned up just a tiny bit. "Are they putting bows in her hair? She really likes that."

Kaia nodded. The lie was easier with just a gesture.

Jessica sighed. "I miss her, too."

"I know this is hard." Kaia pulled her hand back across the table. "And I want to make it end soon."

Jessica shifted in her seat, straightened her shoulders, tossed her hair back, and took a deep breath. Her mouth went back into the severe line everyone was accustomed to, and she tapped at the table with her index finger. "Then you make sure you're recording, because I want everyone to know the truth."

Filled with a rush of exhilaration, Kaia checked her computer to make sure all the little lines of dots were peaking and falling as they should be. Satisfied, she turned back to Jessica.

Jessica waited until she had Kaia's full attention again. For the first time, Veronica squirmed in her chair, making her presence in the room known. But she may as well have been absent since interviewer and interviewee were so deeply focused on one another.

"The truth," Kaia prompted. "What is the truth?"

"He was having an affair and I found out about it. I was done. And it was all I needed to cut him off completely from my money since it violated the pre-nup." Jessica's grin morphed into a smirk. "I even had proof."

Veronica swiveled in her seat, eyes wide. "Proof? Where is this proof?"

Jessica's smug smile melted. "It disappeared along with

Gregory. It was in my roll-top desk in the library. When I sent Tom to get it, he couldn't find it."

"Who's Tom?" Kaia asked.

"Her divorce attorney," Veronica said. "He mentioned the affair to me, but not the proof."

Jessica shrugged, her shoulders flopping. Weeks ago they'd been stiff as hardened steel, now they'd softened under the weight of her burdens. "Hardly matters now. The proof is gone."

Despite Jessica's sense of defeat, Kaia knew what technology could do. Pictures could be retrieved. Emails could be gotten off servers. What was lost could easily be found. "What was the proof?"

"It was a hand-written card. His girlfriend put it with a watch she gave him. I found the card in his freaking underwear drawer." Jessica pointed her finger at Kaia. "And it was good. Really good. It talked about them fucking. It talked about her being in love with him. And it had her damn name signed." Her entire body slumped, her spine curving over the table between them. "But it's gone."

"You know who this woman is? That Gregory was having the affair with?" Kaia asked.

"We know." Veronica said.

Kaia kept her gaze on Jessica and waited. As she expected, the transition in her demeanor occurred again. Jessica sat up, and her eyes grew cold. "Her name is Linda Rosen. I looked her up. She's a sleazy wanna-be model who hangs out at parties with rich people and gets her hooks in men with money."

"Did Gregory know you knew?" Kaia asked.

Jessica shrugged and blinked her eyes.

This kind of reaction did nothing for the recording, so Kaia needed to push. "So you don't know if Gregory knew?"

Jessica shook her head.

Kaia took a deep breath. This was the kind of thing that had the ability to create intense frustration in a podcaster. But she knew she just had to find another path.

Veronica, however, was far less patient. "She needs a verbal answer Jessica." Kaia recognized her words for what they were now—help. In Veronica's mind she was helping Kaia get what she needed and Jessica get what they needed to win her case. Veronica's tone might be cutting, but the daggers came from her heart.

Kaia could have predicted Jessica's reaction to being pushed. She may have chosen the most stubborn attorney on the planet to represent her, but it wasn't because she felt all warm and cozy about her. Kaia suspected Jessica disliked Veronica as much as Veronica disliked her. But Jessica wasn't stupid. She'd taken her family's existing wealth and grown it. She was strategic and cunning, just like Veronica. She probably saw how that was exactly what she needed in court.

Jessica stayed silent.

Kaia shot Veronica a look. To her surprise, Veronica sat back in her seat and gave a terse nod.

Kaia took the conversation back into her own hands. "So you found out he was having an affair. When was this?"

Jessica leaned forward, her elbows splayed out on the table. "A few days before he went missing. Can I ask you a question?"

Kaia's head jerked involuntarily. She'd been in her comfort zone until that moment. The one thing she could count on was that both of the women trapped in this little room with her were usually focused on themselves, allowing her to sneak through the space the way she intended.

With no clue what Jessica was about to ask, Kaia tipped her head.

"Are you a lesbian?"

Kaia let out a breath. That was an easy one. "Yep."

Jessica's mouth curled. "I thought so."

If Jessica wanted to say some stupid, homophobic crap, Kaia could handle that. She'd been shooting back that shit for years. She even knew how to temper the answers for different situations. Someone on the receiving end of her responses—despite the clear mark of their bigotry—rarely pushed any further confrontation.

But Jessica didn't have some snarky quip, instead she dropped an unexpected bomb. "When I get out of here, maybe we could date?"

Before Kaia could wrap her head around this, Veronica's unfiltered mouth entered the discussion. "You like women?"

Jessica shrugged. "Yes." She kept her gaze on Kaia. "And I really like you."

"Thank you," Kaia said. "But I'm seeing someone."

Thirty minutes later, that statement came back to bite her. As soon as they left the jail and slipped into Veronica's car, she pounced. "When you told Jessica that you're dating someone did you mean that girl you were on a date with when I called?"

"Yes. Her."

"So, she's like your girlfriend?"

Kaia took an inordinate amount of time to buckle her seatbelt while she rolled the truth around in her head. She wasn't big on lying, and this wasn't a situation where she could use the excuse of omission since Veronica asked directly. But the real rub was that her view of Veronica had shifted so sharply the night before that she felt compelled to be honest with her now.

"No. We've only been out twice. We haven't had any conversations...it's not serious at the moment. But I didn't see any reason to be that specific with Jessica."

Veronica smiled and turned the key in the ignition. Kaia wondered if she'd just inadvertently opened a door. For some reason, she acknowledged, if she had she wasn't that sorry about it.

Chapter Eleven

There were few things as impressive as Kaia when she was face-to-face with a difficult person like Jessica—or to be honest, Veronica herself. Veronica left that interview all the more impressed with the young woman and filled with a deep, terrible jealousy over the person Kaia was dating.

The ache created this weird new tick. Veronica caught herself rubbing at her sternum regularly. She was doing it again. She stared at her hand briefly, as if to berate it before turning back to her computer. There were things to do.

Kaia had sent a full brief she'd put together on Linda Rosen, making Veronica's contracted PI look like a massive chump. In just twelve hours Kaia had put together a thorough dossier, whereas Brandon was getting a pretty penny and had yet to even delve into this strange side character.

Based on Kaia's research, Linda was as much a piece of work as Jessica claimed. It appeared as though her occupation in life was serial monogamy, and she was getting paid a big salary.

It only took Linda one semester in college to start up a relationship with a professor. She dropped out and lived with him for four years. How that ended wasn't entirely clear, but her address immediately went from his house to that of Bob McKay, a divorced fifty-year old advertising executive with two teenaged kids. She and Bob were married within three months and divorced three years later.

Next on the list was a twenty-six year old tech entrepreneur, her first age match. But despite a five-year relationship, they never got married. In an interview with a magazine, she complained that he couldn't commit. But she still managed to get palimony from him when they split up. The palimony payments dried up when Linda met and quickly married a successful lawyer named Giles Mills.

Veronica's knuckles thumped on her kitchen counter when her hand dropped as quickly as her jaw. She scrolled back up and down again to make sure she'd read that right. Giles Mills? Holy shit!

Giles and Veronica had worked at the same firm together for years. They'd known each other but not been friendly. They weren't enemies, either. He focused on finance law and she occasionally consulted with him about a client's trust fund or life insurance, but it was little more than that. Nevertheless, she had his cell number, and planned to use it.

Before she dialed, Veronica finished reading Kaia's assessment of Linda and Giles's relationship. It ended in divorce a couple years ago and seemed to be the least contentious of all of Linda's court battles over assets and income. But that was all Kaia could find out.

Anxious to get more, Veronica hit the button and waited for a voice to greet her on the line. It didn't take long.

"Hey, Veronica?"

"Yeah. It's me. Hi, Giles."

"Wow. Nice to hear from you. We haven't spoken since you went rogue."

Veronica granted him a tinkling laugh. "Have you missed me?"

"Of course we have. So? To what do I owe the pleasure?"

"I think I forgot that you were married."

A rough chuckle hit the line. "A couple times, why?"

"The last one was Linda Rosen, yeah?"

"Yeah. We're divorced now, though. So what? Oh God, you're not representing her are you?"

"No. No. She didn't kill anyone, as far as I know."

He chuckled again. "Well, I suppose I might be the victim if she did. Why do you ask about Linda?"

"She came up in some research I'm doing."

"She did, huh?"

"Yeah. Do you think we could talk?"

"Absolutely. Let's meet for dinner tomorrow night. I'll text you the details."

Veronica thanked him for taking the time out of his busy schedule and hung up. For some reason she was filled with a strange pride. Perhaps it was the image of her being able to tell Kaia that she'd furthered their pool of knowledge, and that she was a valuable team member after all.

****

When Veronica had suggested the Killer Wit Bistro as an amazing place for an intimate dinner, she'd probably been coming on to Kaia, which gave Kaia a small pain as she sat here now with Lila.

But that little pinprick of guilt was nowhere near as sharp as the pain of this tanking date. The third date being "make or break" was definitely playing itself out in that cozy, little booth tucked tight against the center of the long wall of the narrow restaurant.

"I mean, I just don't like them. They smell, they're dirty, and they drool. And shed! A friend of mine has a dog, and the thing leaves giant clumps of hair all over the place. And I don't just mean on the floor or the couch—which it does—but also on me. If I walk into her house with black pants on, this white dog will make me look like a freaking stuffed polar bear by the time I leave."

Lila was on what seemed like hour two of her rant against dogs, without having paused to so much as ask Kaia if she had a dog. But then it must have occurred to her, because she suddenly paused, tilted her head and said, "Hey, do you have a dog? You never have fur on you, so either you don't or you're a whiz with a lint roller." That beautiful smile lost a little of its shine as Lila flashed it across their table.

Kaia peered at her over the small space packed with wine and water glasses. She shook her head. No point explaining that she was going to get a dog, and that once she did she'd be able to eat more than a plain salad with oil and vinegar dressing at this nice restaurant.

Lila let out a huge sigh. "Good. So, anyway, tell me about your week."

Any desire to talk had fled Kaia just ten minutes into this date when Lila said she wanted the waiter to bring a breadbasket even though Kaia had refused it. The table was now littered with crumbs from the broken rolls Lila had continuously eaten as they nursed their drinks.

Racking her brain for a conversation starter to set Lila onto so she could take over the conversation and Kaia could sit back and endure it, she scanned the restaurant, seeking a suitable subject. Her gaze roamed over a couple in the booth opposite them as well as the trio at a rectangular table running through the center of the slim space.

With neither group providing a hint of interest, she glanced toward the door where a new couple were being led into the main part of the restaurant by the hostess. And that couple stopped Kaia's heart from beating.

Stunning in a silver sheath dress, Veronica's blonde hair cascaded over her shoulders, loose curls bouncing as she walked. Her lips were turned up in a flirty smile as she gazed at the man beside her. Tall, handsome, and a bit older than Veronica, the man moved with her, more focused on Veronica than the hostess leading them to an intimate booth within viewing distance of Kaia and Lila.

Something lurched in Kaia's stomach as the man placed his open palm on Veronica's lower back. An unnamed emotion bubbled up in her chest that caused her breath to come out ragged and uneven.

"What are you looking at?"

Lila's words jolted Kaia out of her intense scrutiny of the newcomers. Kaia whipped her head toward her date and attempted to wipe the emotions off her face. But shock, anger, and that thing she couldn't begin to understand were still ruling her thoughts. "Oh, um. Nothing."

Kaia was too late. Lila followed her gaze just in time to spot Veronica slipping into the booth. "Oh, hey. That's Veronica Turner. You're working with her on the Jessica French case, right?"

Kaia nodded.

"Funny. I think I remember that we saw her dancing on our first date, right?"

Kaia nodded weakly. Her gaze drifted back to Veronica as if a massive magnet tugged on her eyes.

"You didn't even know who she was then," Lila said.

"Nope."

"So, um, who's the guy she's with?"

Kaia turned back to Lila. "I'm not sure."

"They look pretty friendly."

Despite the inexplicable reaction her body was having at the moment, Kaia managed to paste on a casual smile. "Probably a flavor of the week, right?"

Lila chuckled. "Probably. I mean a woman who looks like that should enjoy herself. She probably has 'em lined up."

"Probably. Hey, I need to use the restroom. I'll be right back." Not caring how suspicious it looked, Kaia slid out of the booth and marched directly to Veronica.

As she approached, she could make out the man's last few words. "Is that what you were wondering about?"

Before Veronica could answer him, Kaia cupped her arm around Veronica's upper arm. "Hey. Can we talk?"

Both Veronica and her date dropped open their mouths in shock. Veronica's body was limp, so Kaia used her more powerful muscles to pull her smoothly from the booth. She turned back to the man and said, "We'll be right back."

Veronica didn't utter a sound until Kaia shuffled her into the single-stall all-gender bathroom and the thud of the heavy lock indicated they were alone.

"What the hell?" Veronica shook her arm away from Kaia and took two steps back, essentially pinning herself against the porcelain sink.

"Who is that guy?"

Veronica's eyes flashed. She folded her arms across her chest and leaned toward Kaia. "Why is that any of your business?"

The closest Kaia had ever come to the sensation traveling through her now was a serious fever she'd had when she was fifteen. The way her body burned and her mind stumbled, slow and muddled, was difficult to reconcile with anything other than a sickness.

"Because I want to know."

Veronica straightened up, arms dropping to her sides. Her lips twisted. "Well, I have to say that this demanding, confident side of you is nice to see." She licked her lips, and

Kaia's heart thumped. "But," Veronica tossed her head to force a clump of hair behind her right shoulder, "I don't do double standards."

Kaia scrambled to understand, but she simply couldn't. "Double standard? What do you mean by that?"

"I mean that you don't think I have the right to know shit about your date, who is a freaking gorgeous hottie, by the way. I assume that's the date you mentioned the other day to Jessica, but refused to say shit to me about?" Veronica pointed toward the restaurant. "But you *demand* to know who I am with?"

Kaia had no words to defend herself, because there were none. Veronica was, of course, right. Completely right.

After a few minutes of blank stares, Veronica rolled her eyes, pushed past Kaia and plunged out into the restaurant. Kaia was left reeling, with no choice but to return to her date.

Chapter Twelve

Walking out of that bathroom might have been the hardest thing Veronica ever did. Kaia wanted to know about the man Veronica was with. She practically vibrated with anger. It could only mean one thing: Kaia was jealous.

Veronica's anger was no game. She didn't peddle in guile. Her sense of fairness and justice was absolute, and Kaia had broken that. And while Veronica could no doubt overcome that for Kaia, she had other business to attend to.

Giles's gaze roamed over Veronica as she approached the table. His undisguised desire had never been so apparent when they worked together, but now that they were no longer co-workers, he was unabashed in his interest.

Veronica needed information from Giles, and she was willing to use whatever she needed to get it. More aware of the swing in her hips as she moved, Veronica ensured he got an eyeful as she approached their booth.

She slipped into the slick, wooden seat and sat as far on the edge as she could to allow her a view of Kaia's table. The date waited for Kaia's return as Veronica turned to Giles. She flashed him a smile and rested her hands on the table. "So, we were talking about your ex, Linda."

Giles folded his hands on the table, laying them just inches from hers, and pursed his lips. "So, you're not going to explain that?" He waved toward the bathroom with one hand before slapping his palm back on the table.

Veronica resisted the urge to look behind her to see if Kaia had emerged. She shrugged. "Lady didn't like that I got her ex-girlfriend out of some charges is all. No biggie. Tell me about Linda."

"Tell me, what does she have to do with Jessica French?"

"Off the record?" Veronica winked at him. She didn't really think she had anything to lose by telling him about the affair, but she wanted him to believe she did.

Giles leaned closer. He stroked the back of Veronica's hand with one long finger, tracing the pattern of a light blue vein. "Of course. It's just us talking here."

Veronica used her coy act to slide her gaze to the right and check on the booth that she couldn't stop thinking about. Kaia was back now, chatting animatedly with her date.

Veronica took a deep breath and plunged back into her conversation with Giles. "The thing is, Jessica is convinced that Linda was having an affair with Gregory."

Giles slouched down in the booth suddenly, his back hitting the tall wooden seat with a clap. "What? With Gregory French?"

Veronica nodded and bit her lip. "I'm afraid so."

"Wow."

"You didn't know about this?"

The slightest hesitation preceded Giles's headshake. It was just enough for Veronica to know he was lying.

"So, um. If it were true..." Veronica waited for him to fill in the blanks.

"What? If it were true, what?"

Veronica shrugged. "I mean, do you think it's possible Linda had something to do with Gregory's disappearance?"

The air around the little booth may as well have frozen solid. Giles's eyes narrowed. His chin jerked out. His hands clenched into fists on the solid wood table between them. "Listen to me carefully, Veronica." The jovial voice was gone. What remained was a deep, dark hiss. "I advise you as a colleague and a friend. Do not spend one more minute looking at Linda."

So taken aback by this sudden shift, Veronica stuttered. "Wh-what?"

Giles leaned over the table, his knuckles pressing into the wood. "Do. Not. Look. At. My. Ex. Wife."

"Why not?" Still unable to fathom what had created this level of terrifying evil emanating from Giles, Veronica wanted more. She saw no other course of action. "Why shouldn't I look? She was dating a murder victim, Giles. And my client is being accused of that murder. I don't have any choice but to look into every possibility. And it would be irresponsible of me not to investigate Linda."

Any trace of humanity left his face. Eyes cold and piercing, he leaned forward. He left no room for any misunderstanding. "I'll tell you why you need to leave Linda alone. Because you'll be sorry." He grabbed her hand and pressed it into the cold tabletop. "Lane and I have become close since you left, you know. I know what scares you. I know what gets you on your knees and begging. I will hurt you."

Before Veronica could even breathe, Giles stormed out of the booth. His departure was so quick it was almost as if he'd teleported away from her, the restaurant, and the entire conversation.

Veronica's need to feel safe overrode any sense of anger she'd felt just ten minutes before. Now she was left with a familiar feeling, one Lane had instilled in her. Her instinct was to immediately seek out safety. For reasons she couldn't fully analyze at that moment, Kaia meant safety.

She pulled herself up and stumbled toward the booth she'd been intent to keep an eye on earlier, catapulting herself toward the strong, quiet woman. But the booth was empty. Kaia was gone. And she was alone.

****

Veronica's name lit up her cell and created a whirlwind of emotions so complex Kaia had no choice but to send the call directly to voicemail. She'd been home no more than fifteen minutes after her disastrous date. That it had gone poorly since before Veronica walked into the restaurant seemed irrelevant now, because it completely tanked after their confrontation in the ladies' room.

There was no amount of wine and small talk that could inflate Kaia's mood. With Veronica just a few feet away, she knew there would be no way to carry on any kind of conversation with Lila. Lila seemed relieved when Kaia suggested they leave. She was less pleased when they got outside and Kaia ended the date altogether.

She managed to get settled on a yoga mat in the center of her living room and get her breathing where it needed to be before the incessant ringing of the phone told her everything was still a hot mess. Kaia stared at the cell phone for several long beats. Her fingers gripped it as if it were a rope and she were dangling off a cliff.

The deep dive she'd taken tonight when she'd seen Veronica was not unlike a great fall. It would take time and reflection, and probably a ton of meditation to figure it all out.

But that phone call. Less than an hour had passed since their confrontation. That wasn't much time, given Veronica had just entered the restaurant when Kaia waltzed up to her and shoved her into that bathroom. What could have happened that could have led to a call now? Was she still on her date? Was she hiding in the bathroom calling Kaia?

She told herself she needed more time to unravel her feelings, but that rationale wouldn't win the argument against her curiosity. Which is why when the phone indicated a voicemail, she immediately pressed play.

"Hey, it's Veronica. Um. I..." The pause, deep and significant, amplified the stress echoing through Veronica's voice. "I think I have a problem. And I'm a little freaked out. And I...was hoping..." A heavy breath hit the phone as if Veronica hadn't exhaled in hours. "It doesn't matter. Call me if you want."

Kaia's chest tightened. There was no hint of manipulation in the tenor of Veronica's voice, just sheer terror. Before her heart could retain a steady beat again, she dialed.

After one ring, Veronica's voice echoed on the line. "Kaia?"

"Where are you?"

An excruciating pause had Kaia shooting up, her knees popping as she reached a standing position, bare feet creating indents in the yoga mat.

"Hi, Kaia." Veronica's voice came through the line less terrified than it was on the message, but soft, way too soft. "I'm at Malcolm's place."

"What happened? What's wrong?"

"Can you come here and I'll tell you all about it? It's

not far, the high rise on the corner of your street and Golden Gate."

Kaia didn't stop to think. She told Veronica she'd be there in a few minutes, put on her shoes, and bolted out the door.

Chapter Thirteen

The elevator ride lasted at least three years. Going up nineteen stories was disconcerting anyway, but the distance from Veronica and the painful amount of time it took to get to her nearly undid Kaia.

When the shiny metal doors of the elevator finally slid open, she lunged through them and into a thickly carpeted corridor. The dark wood doors on either side, marked with brass numbers, made the building look more like a hotel on the Embarcadero than a large apartment building at the edge of Hayes Valley.

The door to Malcolm's apartment opened before she reached it. Malcolm stepped into the corridor, a beautiful Australian Shepherd at his heels. His bright brown eyes softened and his shoulders relaxed as she approached. "Kaia. Thank you for coming."

Kaia didn't have time for much more than a nod and a weak smile thrown at Malcolm. She followed him into his apartment, her short legs moved quickly to keep up with his much longer ones. A narrow hallway opened up into a boxy living room and kitchen combination area, flanked on one end by floor-to-ceiling windows with a view of the city.

On the couch, which was pressed against one wall, Veronica sat like a terrified kitten, her back resting on a large square pillow, her legs tucked up under her butt. Her face ashen, her eyes wide and red.

Drawn to her, Kaia folded herself into the space beside Veronica while Malcolm ducked into the kitchen, the upper part of his body showing above the island sink.

"Hey, there," Kaia said gently.

Veronica's hands moved from their place in her lap toward Kaia. But as if she caught herself, Veronica abruptly pulled them back, clutching them to her own chest instead. "Thanks for coming."

"Of course. Are you okay?"

Veronica shook her head sending golden locks of hair swooping around her neck and shoulders.

Kaia's heart shattered. "What happened?"

"That guy you saw me with at the restaurant, he's an attorney. I used to work with him."

Kaia swallowed down all the unresolved issues about what happened between them, focusing on Veronica's story and what she needed to get out. "The firm you used to work for?"

Veronica nodded. The action caused one of those shiny locks of hair to fall across her cheek and stick to the wet track of a recently shed tear. "We weren't really close. We didn't work together much. He does a lot of finance stuff."

Kaia nodded, hoping it would encourage her to continue. But Veronica's bright blue eyes left Kaia's face as she watched Malcolm move toward them. He placed a glass of ice water on the coffee table beside a half-filled one before settling into a chair opposite the two women.

"So, this guy?" Kaia prompted.

Veronica's gaze slid back to Kaia. "Giles. I called him because Linda Rosen is his ex-wife."

Kaia had the research about Linda, but she hadn't put Giles together with Veronica. She nearly hit herself on the forehead for not connecting those dots. "Yeah. And he agreed to meet you?"

"Yes, but it wasn't romantic," Veronica said. "I wanted to get information on the case."

The confession hit Kaia like a freight train packed with guilt. "I see."

"I asked him about Linda and her involvement with Gregory French." Veronica stopped at this, as if continuing her story had suddenly become very hard.

Kaia placed one hand on Veronica's thigh "What did he say?"

"He threatened me. Told me to leave it be or I'd be sorry." Veronica's eyes were enormous.

It was almost unfathomable to imagine this warrior woman in such a state of terror. Now, faced with it in the most raw state, Kaia felt cold to her bones. This was not right, not at all.

She glanced toward Malcolm. His own face was crumpled in concern, but his body was relaxed, reflecting what Kaia assumed was a belief that Veronica was completely safe in his presence.

"So she's staying here?" Kaia asked Malcolm.

His demeanor changed the moment the question left her lips. "Well, I have to leave early tomorrow," his lips twisted, "at 5 a.m. to catch a flight."

Kaia moved her gaze back toward Veronica. A miserable expression painted her beautiful features. She was afraid, and the savior she'd chosen had no choice but to leave her in less than eight hours.

Kaia's decision was swift and irrational. "She can stay with me."

****

Few things could create this level of discomfort in Veronica. Being a trembling, vulnerable mess in front a non-family member—an attractive, deeply interesting one at that—was definitely on the list.

Her fear was far less embarrassing in front of Malcolm. He was family. He'd seen some of her most horrific childhood moments, including all of her dance recitals, and that time she agreed to dress up as the snow queen in a local play. It was different with Kaia. Veronica wanted Kaia's attention in every way—but not like this. Not in a moment of deep anxiety that was a product of her own stupid life decisions.

"This is my favorite," Kaia said, handing Veronica a thick, cream-colored mug filled with steaming liquid.

Veronica took the mug and cradled it in both of her hands as Kaia dropped into the seat beside her on the overstuffed couch. Her gaze roamed the warm, cozy room and wondered again how she'd ended up in Kaia's home. "Thank you. What is it?"

Kaia smiled, making Veronica's stomach quiver uncomfortably. "It's a hot toddy. It's mostly sweet and smooth with a touch of alcohol to take the edge off. Drink up."

Veronica took a tentative sip and found it to be as perfect as Kaia had described it. A small hum escaped her throat. "Family recipe?"

Kaia chuckled softly. "Yeah. It is. And it's a secret. I could tell you what's in it, but I'd have to kill you." A brilliant smile accompanied her quip, forcing Veronica's shoulders to settle lower and her breath to come easier.

Veronica, compelled to take another sip, exhaled and closed her eyes. "This is perfect."

A soft hand landed on Veronica's knee. "I'm glad."

Veronica stared at that hand, the warmth flowing from it penetrating every part of her terrified body. "Thank you for taking me home." The words were wrong, not quite what she meant. But in that moment they were completely honest, and that was the best she could do.

"I think," Kaia hesitated. Veronica tore her gaze from where Kaia's hand sat on her knee to Kaia's liquid, brown eyes. Only then did Kaia finish her thought. "I think things have changed between us enough that you don't need to thank me."

"I don't?"

Kaia shook her head. Tendrils of soft brown hair whipped around her temple. "We're friends now, right?"

"Are we?"

Kaia frowned. "Where's my Veronica? The one who would say—hell yeah, we are, bitch. Where did she go?"

The little phrase "*my* Veronica" tilted the axis of her world. But there were bigger issues at play. Veronica had to either snap herself out of this fear-induced funk and bring back the lively woman that Kaia wanted to see, or allow her insides to be exposed even further.

It would be easier to be stripped naked, left on an island with a stranger and filmed while she tried to survive. Veronica abruptly got up from the couch, ripped herself away from Kaia and made a beeline for the nearest door. She hoped it was either a bathroom or a bedroom. She needed a minute alone to gather herself.

It wasn't until she was fully inside with the door closed

securely behind her that she realized she'd plunged straight into a large storage closet. Shelves packed with towels, blankets, spare pillows, and neatly folded clothes, as well as coats, boots, and a pair of skis all sat in judgment of her epic faux pas.

An involuntary tear escaped as hopelessness, punctuated by extreme embarrassment, racked her. If Kaia wanted to be friends with the sharp-tongued, brazen attorney, she surely wouldn't want anything to do with the melting puddle of cowardice in the closet. And since Veronica wanted much more from Kaia than friendship, her failure was all the more poignant.

In the midst of her intense emotional moment, it occurred to Veronica that there was another aspect to her situation. Her desire for Kaia was a sexual realization, and now she was trapped in a closet.

Veronica laughed, the bark so loud it echoed off the close walls of the tiny space. The laugh prompted more, and she ended up in a fit of hysterics, tears of mirth streaming down her face.

Doubled over, her head on a fluffy blue towel, she barely noticed the door behind her open. She turned to see Kaia standing in the doorway. But it didn't stop the laughing. It seemed nothing could halt that train as it barreled down the track.

Kaia stayed silent as Veronica gradually began to calm down. When her breath came in rough pants, Kaia's hand fell on her back, soft and strong. Veronica chased that sensation, turning to fall into Kaia. She was taller, but her face fit perfectly into the crook of Kaia's neck and shoulder as she bent over.

Kaia's warm arms wrapped around Veronica's waist. Veronica sunk into the embrace, no longer caring about her embarrassment, her need to be strong in front of the woman she was deeply attracted to, or her existential crisis.

"Come on," Kaia said softly. "Let's go sit down."

Veronica let Kaia pull her into the living room. They both sank onto the couch and gravitated toward each other, meeting in the center as if a special dip—created just for them—were built into the furniture.

Calm spread through Veronica like gentle waves slowly wetting the dry beach sand during high tide. She abandoned the turbulent emotions inside her, laid her head on Kaia's shoulder and closed her eyes.

A gentle hand squeezed her thigh just above the knee—that perfect place where a tiny bit of pressure had the ability to radiate through the body. Veronica released a heavy breath that stirred up a lock of long, blonde hair that brushed her cheek lightly before landing on her neck.

"You gonna tell me what's so funny?"

An unexpected snort escaped Veronica that only started another, much shorter, round of giggles. "I was in the closet, thinking about how I'd been in the closet for years."

"Hmmm. That is a bit of an amusing coincidence."

Veronica glanced up at Kaia. Her expression was unreadable. "What are you thinking?" As soon as the words left her mouth, she regretted them. What if Kaia told her she was thinking that the hot mess of a woman in her arms was not the strong ball-buster she'd begun to like?

"I was wondering why you went into the closet in the first place. The real one, not the figurative one."

Veronica settled her head back on Kaia's shoulder and closed her eyes. "Fear."

"Of me?"

Veronica's head snapped up again. "You? No."

"Well, Giles has no idea I exist. You're safe from him here. So what were you afraid of?"

"Me."

"Hmmm." The soft sound coming from the back of Kaia's throat soothed Veronica. She settled back against the couch, still relaxed, still touching Kaia, but able to gaze into those deep, brown eyes.

"Well, you can't run from that."

The statement—said with a mixture of understanding, wisdom, and sympathy—drove into Veronica's soul. Never had anyone said anything so perfectly true.

Beats of time passed like the drumming of surf on the shore. Veronica stared into Kaia's eyes and knew everything had changed. "Will you kiss me?" The question was more plea than question, said in the softest, meekest voice

Veronica had ever used.

Kaia didn't speak, instead she shifted on the couch and brought them face-to-face. She cupped Veronica's cheeks in her hands, drifting slowly toward her. Their lips met with a feather-light touch at first. The contact was pure warmth and comfort.

Veronica stayed still, too insecure to allow her body any agency. So when Kaia pressed closer—opening her lips and licking gently—tension flowed out of Veronica, and she invited Kaia in.

Chapter Fourteen

The beautiful blonde snored, an adorable soft, kitten-esque sound. From her position on the loveseat—that was plenty big for her short self to curl up on—Kaia had a great view of Veronica.

When Veronica had first fallen asleep last night on the long couch in the center of Kaia's living room, she was curled up, using less than half the full length of the fluffy piece of furniture. But this morning she was stretched out, her stocking feet barely grazing the arm of the couch. She lay on her back, one arm hanging off the edge, hand just barely touching the carpet.

Veronica's face was soft, lips slightly parted, eyelashes floating just above the pale skin below her eyes. In that moment, having just been awakened by the sun that streamed through the large bay window behind her, Kaia knew she'd never seen anything so beautiful in her life.

An ache crept into her chest. Nothing about that kiss last night was the right thing to do, even though it felt that way in the moment. Veronica was vulnerable. She needed a friend. But Kaia had let her own desire take over the moment "kiss me" came out of Veronica's mouth.

Now shame colored that moment. An intense fire burned in Kaia's belly for Veronica. But the woman was scared, and clearly in the middle of working through her shit. Kaia didn't need to confuse the issue or make it worse with her own blossoming want.

As Kaia watched, a beam of light skipped over her shoulder to land directly on Veronica's left eye. Graceful arms stretched above her head, and that luscious mouth parted in a wide yawn.

Before Veronica's blue eyes could open and pierce Kaia's guilty soul, she pulled herself off the loveseat and hurried to the kitchen. It took forever to get the coffee percolating because she usually took at least twenty minutes to coax herself out of bed. Having bolted up so quickly seemed to have filled her brain with cotton.

While the coffeemaker gurgled and bubbled, Kaia pulled out the ingredients she needed to make a veggie omelet and hash browns, careful to avoid peeking past the island that separated the living room and kitchen.

Once the potatoes were sizzling in the cast iron skillet and all the ingredients for an incredible omelet were diced and ready, she allowed her gaze to land on the island. Veronica sat, slumped and tired, but glorious, on a stool facing her.

"Morning," Kaia mumbled. Instead of waiting for a reply to her greeting, she ducked down to pull her favorite pan for making eggs out of a low cabinet.

"Hi." Veronica's soft voice hit her ears like velvet on skin. "Can I help?"

"No. No." Kaia stood straight, the pan brandished in her hand. "You want coffee?"

Veronica nodded. "Please."

As she prepared a cup with the requested dab of cream, Kaia reflected on how vastly different the woman at her kitchen island was from the one she'd confronted in the bathroom of the restaurant the evening before.

She placed her favorite Rosie the Riveter mug in front of her guest with a smile she hoped was comforting. If her expression reflected the conflict within her, it wouldn't provide the reassurance Veronica needed.

"Thank you for taking me in," Veronica said.

Turned, with her profile to Veronica, Kaia's focus stayed on prepping the pan for her breakfast masterpiece. "No problem."

"My parents can't know about any of this. They're just...very overprotective, and my dad's heart is bad. Anyway, Malcolm will be back tomorrow. So..."

"No problem. You can stay as long as you need." Kaia glanced quickly at Veronica before turning back to her work. "I actually have extra sheets and blankets. I guess we just never got to that last night." She forced herself to chuckle casually. Any mention of the night before was dangerous territory.

"I don't know how long I need to stay away from home," Veronica said. "Or even if I do." She ran a hand through her hair. "He knows where I live is all...and anyway, I'm going to the prosecutor's office this morning."

Kaia slipped the last ingredient into her pan, turned down the heat, and placed a lid on top. Then she swung around to face Veronica. "How are you feeling about that? Going to see the prosecutor, I mean."

Veronica shrugged. "Matt's a friend. I'd rather just have a conversation with him than file a police report. Though, he'll want me to do that." She ran her finger over a spot on the counter, frowning at it. "Still...I can't help but wonder if I'm over-reacting?"

Kaia dropped her hands, palms open, onto the countertop. "No. Stop."

Veronica's head snapped up. So much uncertainty reflected back to Kaia in those warm eyes she once thought of as cold and calculating.

"Would you tell a client that if she were in your shoes?" Kaia asked.

Veronica's teeth trapped her bottom lip. Her eyes roamed Kaia's face. The unexpected moisture shining there melted Kaia's heart as if it were a wax candle. After a long beat, Veronica spoke, her voice soft and unsure. "No, I wouldn't."

"Right." Kaia smacked the counter as she stood.

Grateful that Veronica's answer gave her the excuse to turn away, she moved to the stove. For a while the clanging of dishes and utensils filled the room as Kaia served up breakfast.

Kaia slid Veronica's plate to her. Without making eye contact, Veronica took it, her focus solely on the food. Kaia's legs instinctively tried to carry her around the island to sit in her normal seat. But she hesitated, then stood in the kitchen and ate her breakfast there, rather than put herself within inches of her guest.

A deep, penetrating silence drifted between and around the two women. Their gazes fluttered about the room, landing everywhere but on each other. Kaia shifted her stance and attempted to wipe the sweat from her palms on her jeans.

An impulsive desire to flee rose in her chest and pressed on her like a weight. It forced her hand. When she'd finished eating, she didn't even bother to wash the dishes, she just stuck them all in the sink and bolted to the front door.

Kaia looked over her shoulder briefly. "I…uh…have a thing. Good luck with the A.D.A."

Veronica shot her a shy smile that Kaia just barely caught before she closed the door behind her.

****

Matt was playing a political game Veronica knew all too well. And even though it was her life and her safety on the line, the ruse created a sense of challenge that brought out Veronica's tigress. It was exactly what she needed at that moment. To feel like herself again. To fight and challenge. It created a rush that overwhelmed her fear and anxiety.

"I've invited Detective Poll to join us, so we can assure you that your concerns are met with positive action on our part." As if he were a game show host, Matt splayed out his arm and gestured toward Poll, who sat beside him.

Veronica sat in the center of the long, polished table with a sea of empty chairs to her right and left. The two men, both in starched shirts and tightly knotted ties, sat opposite her. The set-up was meant to intimidate, but it had no such effect on her.

Veronica stared into Poll's eyes and took a moment to remind him that their previous encounters were not forgotten. "Detective Poll, we meet again." She turned back to the prosecutor. "I appreciate your consideration."

"He's our best." Matt's toothy smile was just as sparkling white and just as irritating as it was when he'd mentored her class in law school.

Veronica cocked her head as if to lay doubt on this statement. She felt fully entitled to do so. After Detective Poll falsely suspected Dr. Helen Nims of murder, Veronica was completely vindicated in her defense of the woman.

Poll said nothing. Matt cleared his throat before continuing on his sunshine and rose path. "I understand you're concerned about a former colleague?"

"Giles Mills threatened me last night."

Matt threw his head back in an overdramatic display of surprise. "Giles Mills. The estate attorney? He hardly seems like the type—"

"Giles Mills isn't some quiet number cruncher, Matt. He's in criminal law. It just so happens that he has carved out a niche for himself taking care of the funds of people who are on trial. It shows he's ambitious, not that he's harmless."

Matt scrunched his eyebrows together. "Why would he threaten you? Over you leaving the firm?"

"No. He threatened me because I asked questions about his ex-wife, Linda Rosen."

"I don't follow."

"I do." Detective Poll spoke for the first time since Veronica entered the room. "She is rumored to have had an affair with your client's missing husband."

Veronica examined him. The shiny spot created by his male-pattern baldness reflected back at her. Complex hazel eyes pierced her from beneath a set of bushy grey eyebrows. He was the type of man who looked like he'd seen it all, and probably had.

Veronica nodded tersely. "That's right. I discovered that she was Giles's ex. Since he and I know each other, I asked to meet up with him. We went to dinner and when I asked questions about her, he threatened me."

"What—exactly—did he say?"

Veronica ignored Matt's condescending tone. There was no way in hell she was exposing her own deep, dark secret to Matt now that he was showing his true colors. So she kept it simple. She left out the way Giles had mentioned Lane. "He said if I continued to look into his ex-wife I'd be sorry."

"That's it? You'd be sorry." Matt had the gall to actually laugh.

Veronica slowly pulled in a breath, willing the heat in

her blood to cool.

Detective Poll spoke, his voice smooth and calm, "I'm guessing that the way he said those words, and the way he looked when he said them was what made them threatening, yes?"

To keep herself from smacking the smirk off Matt's face, Veronica focused on Poll. "That's exactly right. I'm not ashamed to tell you that I was—that I am—terrified. I didn't go home last night."

Detective Poll nodded. "Wise choice. Are you staying somewhere for a few days?"

Veronica's brain flashed to Kaia. Unwilling to get distracted, she tore her thoughts away from the kind woman and her warm kiss. "Yes."

Poll nodded solemnly.

"Oh, come on. All this over, *you'll be sorry*. And coming from a respected lawyer. Don't you think this is an over-reaction?"

Veronica hit Matt with her "if-looks-could-kill" gaze. "No. I don't. And apparently, neither does the detective." She nodded toward Poll.

"Look. I understand that threats are often more than they seem." Matt smoothed his tie and tightened up his tone. "But we're talking about fairly innocuous words said in a very public setting. Right? In a restaurant? Or was this in some dark alley or something?"

Knowing her own temper the way she did, Veronica stood. She moved the chair behind her, rolling it smoothly so that it crashed into the one to her right. She took a step back, the click of her heels on the hardwood floor gave her a sense of power. "I think I've had enough. I suppose I'll file a police report and watch that go nowhere. But at least it will be written down."

She spun toward the door but stopped when she heard Poll's voice. "I'll take that report myself."

Veronica turned around. Poll stood as well, making the still seated prosecutor look small and mean in his chair. A contrast made even greater when Matt squinted up at him. "That's not your job."

Poll stepped around the table to open the door for

Veronica. "It is today."

Chapter Fifteen

It had been three days since Veronica spent the night on her couch. Three days since their kiss and the awkward morning after. There hadn't been a second night. No time to reconcile all that happened. Instead, Malcolm returned early from his trip, scooped Veronica up and whisked her off to his place.

Kaia and Veronica hadn't spoken since. There were texts, though—lots of them. They started after Veronica met with the prosecutor. It hadn't gone well, that much was clear from the texts.

Kaia wished Veronica had called her so she could give her more than a few words typed on a screen. At the same time, she was relieved for the less personal communication. Everything was like that with them. Kaia wanted more, but also less.

The texts continued. Most of them were benign. Veronica told Kaia that Malcolm had returned early and she'd be staying with him, not her. Kaia checked in with Veronica only to learn that she and Malcolm had shared a couple bottles of wine and were playing a very ridiculous game of Risk.

But the text exchange that led to this exact moment almost never got sent. Kaia typed it quickly. "Agnes and Helen are back with the baby. Wanna meet her? Come to my house tonight."

It would only be a matter of time before Veronica met the kid anyway. But Kaia hadn't written the text out of urgency for that introduction. She'd sent it because she missed Veronica.

That realization hit the moment she'd pushed the little button ushering that text flying out into the universe to land squarely on Veronica's phone. Kaia missed the attorney, who was a bundle of contradictions and a thorn in her side.

Now Veronica sat opposite Helen, Agnes, and toddler Jackie at her kitchen table while Kaia finished making dinner. Conversation, laughter, and baby talk all floated back to her. A surprising amount of all three came from Veronica, who finally seemed to relax after her ordeal with the creepy ex-co-worker.

All three women avoided the subject of Giles Mills, and even Jessica and the case altogether. Instead, every conversation centered around Jackie, her sad story, her adorableness, and the journey her new parents had taken to get her.

Kaia smiled to herself as she taste-tested the sangria she'd made to go with her Spanish-inspired dinner. It was perfect in flavor as well as perfectly suited for such a joyous occasion. They could use a little light in their lives.

She stacked the pitcher and glasses onto a vintage tray that featured a large lemon cut into slices. The pitcher was faded but beloved, nonetheless. Every time Kaia used it, she thought of summer afternoons at her grandparents' farm in Ohio.

As soon as Kaia swung around the island with the tray in her hand, Veronica jumped up from her seat at the table. "Can I help?"

Kaia smiled and handed her the tray. "Sure. If you'll get everyone drinks, I'll go back and get dinner."

Veronica's answering smile was radiant. The tender way her eyes lit up nearly undid Kaia. "I can't wait. It smells amazing."

Helen and Agnes added to the conversation, but whatever they said was lost in Kaia's muddled mind. She'd been unable to think straight in Veronica's presence since that confrontation in the restaurant bathroom. And the ailment didn't seem to be getting any better.

Safely back in the kitchen, Kaia turned her back to her guests and took three measured breaths, counting to ten as she slowly exhaled each one. Something remarkable and terrifying was happening to her.

She plastered on a casual grin and carried the rest of the meal out to the waiting women. Once everything was arranged on the rickety folding table Kaia used only for special occasions, she had no choice but to the take the remaining seat.

Four chairs normally fit comfortably around the small square, but with a highchair squeezed in for Jackie, the fit was tighter. It brought Kaia so close to Veronica as she sat down that their knees brushed. She immediately pulled away and knocked her opposite knee into Helen's on the other side.

Kaia knew the flush that rose from her neck to her cheeks had to be obvious, despite her light brown skin. She stared at the food as she took several more deep breaths. Conversation floated around her as if there wasn't a fog of static, awkward air that hung over the table nearly suffocating everyone under its influence.

Kaia ate in relative silence. After the first few questions tossed to her by Agnes or Helen were answered with monosyllabic responses, they stopped trying. It wasn't until dinner was eaten and the four women sat around the table piled with empty plates, that Kaia could no longer avoid conversation.

All eyes in the room were on little Jackie. One chubby cheek was smooshed against Agnes's chest. Long, delicate eyelashes fanned over soft skin above her cheeks. Little puffs of air escaped her rosy lips as she slept.

"Kaia, how are you really?" Agnes asked.

Kaia pulled her gaze up to Agnes. "I'm good. Things are going well with the podcast."

"Not the podcast. You. How are you?"

Kaia's gaze involuntarily shifted to Veronica. "I'm okay."

"Kaia and I haven't spoken since the night she took me in," Veronica said, her own gaze piercing back.

"Sure we have," Kaia protested.

Veronica rolled her eyes. The action—somehow sweet and intimate—had Kaia's heart in her throat again. "Texts don't count."

"I see," Agnes said.

"Me, too." Helen rose from her seat. She moved to the couch where Jackie's diaper bag was spilled out like a fountain of baby debris. She quickly shoved everything into the vessel and slung it over her shoulder. "It was lovely seeing you both, but we're going to have to insist that you talk this out."

"Wait. What? You're leaving?" Kaia asked.

"Yes. But you're going to get started while we get ready." Agnes glanced up at Helen. "We have a diaper to change."

Helen sighed and dropped the bag back on the couch. "We need to get her potty trained soon."

"Soon, baby. Let's get her adjusted first." Agnes turned to Kaia and Veronica. "Into the bedroom with you both." Agnes pointed her finger toward the hallway. "Go."

Veronica must have felt the command as deeply as Kaia did, because neither of them argued as they marched into Kaia's bedroom. Veronica closed the door as Kaia turned to face her.

Maybe six feet was all that remained as open space in Kaia's small bedroom. The bed took up the majority of the room, her dresser and bedside table occupying what was left. A small rug lay in front of the sliding closet doors, its brown and blue paisley pattern the only walking space available.

That's where they stood now, one on each side of that little rug, staring at each other with equally large eyes and open mouths.

"I shouldn't have kissed you the other night," Kaia said. "I'm sorry for that."

Veronica cocked her head. "You're sorry you did it?"

"No. I mean," she took a deep breath, "I'm sorry if it was the wrong thing to do."

"Why was it the wrong thing to do?"

Warmth spread through Kaia. She felt as if she were being interrogated under one of those bright yellow lamps. She ran a sweaty hand through her hair. "Well, wasn't it?"

Veronica took a step forward, closing the space between them on that tiny rug. "Why? Because you didn't mean it? Because you didn't like it?"

"No. No. I meant it, and I liked it."

Veronica smiled so wide little dimples popped up in her cheeks. "Yeah?"

Kaia let out a breath. "But you were so..." She stopped herself from saying vulnerable. That word was probably like kryptonite to a woman like Veronica. She understood that about her now. "It just seemed like the wrong time."

Veronica took another step forward. "When is the right time?"

With less than a foot between them, Kaia had nowhere to go. The sensation of being trapped lasted for a fleeting moment before it was replaced by something else. The heat of embarrassment and confusion morphed into the burning fire of desire. But Kaia resisted the urge to lean forward and take Veronica's lips in hers. "I'm not sure."

"But there is, in fact, a good time, right?"

In no mood for games, Kaia asked for plain speech. "What do you mean?"

Veronica inched closer, her lips now just inches away. "I mean...did you change your mind? That there is a good time? That I have a shot with you?"

Those sky-blue eyes beckoned Kaia forward. She had no choice but to obey. Not certain how to answer Veronica's questions, Kaia responded with a searing kiss.

****

Veronica's brain barely registered Helen's voice call out that they were leaving. How she was able to comprehend that distant sound when Kaia's lips were sealed to her own was a mystery she'd never unravel.

Instinct controlled Veronica's movements as she led Kaia down onto the bed. It felt amazing. Kaia gave way under her until they were all the way down, Veronica's torso completely covering her.

But the dynamic changed quickly. The shorter Kaia was a million times stronger, her toned arms accustomed to hoisting heavy equipment. She leveraged that strength to roll them both over, so Kaia was on top.

It was even better like this. Veronica's entire being buzzed. Excitement, desire, and peace battled for the greatest part of her attention. But all slipped away from her focus. Consumed with all things Kaia, she noted the fresh scent—not unlike that of an herb garden after a cleansing rain—the strong hands sliding down her ribs, and the gentle weight of a curvy, voluptuous body pressing on her own.

A part of Veronica's brain found the space to contemplate why it was that this moment was so much more sensual, so deeply intimate, and so intensely better than any other sexual moment in her life. She found no immediate answer to the puzzle, and abandoned the quest.

She concentrated on swimming in the sensations Kaia created with her strong, yet gentle, touch. Fingers found their way just beyond the waistband of her cotton skirt, a flouncy thing she'd chosen for this casual get together that now seemed completely in the way. But Kaia was undeterred by the material, her soft fingertips grasped Veronica's hip in a way that was at the same time hesitant and possessive.

An involuntary groan escaped Veronica's throat, the vibration reaching up to where their mouths were joined. She nearly panicked when the sound caused Kaia to pull back, leaving her bereft.

Kaia's dark eyes roamed her face. "Are you good?"

"So good." Throaty and cracking, her voice reflected how wrecked she was in that moment.

"You sure?"

Veronica pressed the heel of her hand into Kaia's back, willing her to return to the position she craved. "So sure. Please." The plea was breathless and needy, two things Veronica was certain she'd never been before in her life.

Despite Veronica's belief that she was surely a pathetic being, Kaia didn't laugh, or smile. She didn't smirk or make a comment about how great she must be at kissing, all things Veronica might have expected of her ex, were he capable of creating this reaction in her.

Instead, Kaia licked her lips, eyes piercing Veronica, before diving back into a passionate kiss.

****

Kaia gave in to every instinct she'd been fighting as she made love to Veronica. She shed all her doubt about her ability to be the kind of woman someone like Veronica needed. She dropped every bit of personal baggage that warned her not to trust such a powerful, self-confident person. She peeled away the fear of falling hard for someone who might not be able to give her whole self to Kaia.

The voices that rose in her head, alongside the attraction to Veronica, all fell silent as soon as their lips touched. With Veronica beneath her, soft and pliant, they seemed a million miles away.

Those voices didn't return as she lay, sticky and naked, across her bed with Veronica sprawled beside her, head resting on Kaia's upper arm, as if it were a pillow designed just for her. Her own cheek touched the top of Veronica's silky, blonde hair.

Kaia ran her free hand leisurely along Veronica's slim waist and bumpy ribs. "You okay?"

"I don't think I've ever been more okay in my life." Veronica sighed deeply. She reached out to touch the top of Kaia's bare thigh and squeezed. "My God. That was incredible."

"Hmmm." Kaia's contented hum served as her only response.

"I can't believe I got to be with you," Veronica said in a near whisper. "It's like I'm dreaming."

Kaia huffed. "I'm hardly worth dreaming about."

"I couldn't disagree more."

Kaia dropped a kiss on the top of her head. "Well, you certainly are…you're amazing."

"I never thought we'd be here." Veronica threw the comment out there as if she were reminiscing to herself.

"Me neither."

"Can I ask you something?"

"Of course."

"Where do we go from here?"

Kaia rolled the question around in her head. Bathed in the glow of sex and cuddling, it was hard to look at anything objectively. She felt muddled and soft. The only answer that came to her mind was *More. We do more.* But she didn't say that aloud. Instead, she asked a question of her own, one whose answer was intensely important to Kaia. "Where do you want to go?"

"Can we...can we be together? I mean, will you stay?" The question stood there like a symbol of the vulnerability Veronica held deep beneath her hard exterior.

Kaia searched through her own box of doubt and insecurity, but it had all been emptied. It left along with the voices as they faded away while she took refuge in Veronica's body. Now there was nothing left to stand in their way. "Yes. Yes, I will."

Chapter Sixteen

"You should pay attention. You need to learn to cook." Kaia pointed a wooden spoon across the island at the beautiful blonde perched on a barstool.

Veronica's eyes raked up and down Kaia's body. "Oh, I'm paying attention. Why don't you show me the salad spinner again?"

Kaia narrowed her eyes. She loved the way Veronica teased her, but she'd never let on. "You only want me for my body."

"Baby, I want you for everything that you are."

The statement shifted the atmosphere in the room. The playful tone that had persisted as Kaia worked to create a gourmet dinner and Veronica watched while sipping slowly on a glass of wine, instantly morphed into something far more serious.

Kaia dropped the spoon, leaned over and rested her arms, from elbow to wrist, on the counter between them. Veronica slid her wine glass to the side and mirrored Kaia's action, which brought them so close their noses nearly touched.

Kaia wove her fingers with Veronica's. "It's been a pretty amazing two weeks."

Veronica nodded, her eyes wide and slightly damp. "It really has. Feels longer. Glad you decided to like me."

"It took me a minute to stop being afraid of you." Kaia softened her truthful statement with a light kiss on Veronica's lips.

Veronica frowned. "Sorry I'm scary."

Kaia gave her another quick kiss to lessen the sting. "Didn't I tell you I find the tigress incredibly sexy?"

Veronica grinned. "Actually, you did. Last night as I recall."

Kaia nodded. "Damn right." She stood up but didn't

move away from the counter. She was pinned down by Veronica's expression that clearly indicated she had more to say.

"Next Sunday is family dinner." No mirth remained in Veronica's sky-blue eyes. She was as serious now as she was in a courtroom. "Will you come? As my date?"

Despite having become familiar with it, the hint of insecurity in the powerful woman's tone still baffled Kaia. How it could be Kaia, of all people, made a person like Veronica—otherwise so utterly filled with confidence—wonder about her impact, she wasn't certain.

Kaia wanted nothing more than to provide Veronica with a blanket of comfort. "Of course, I will."

"I'll do my best to keep my family from embarrassing you. No guarantees though." Veronica smiled shyly.

That Veronica understood, in a way few others did, her deep-seated issues with eating and the way the food going into her mouth always became the center of attention from well-meaning people was a comfort Kaia had never known from a lover before.

The affection that rose so easily in her chest when she was near Veronica had her lean forward for another kiss. But midway to her goal she was startled by the tinkling ring of her cell phone. Kaia straightened quickly and fished the phone out of the front pocket of her shirt. She slammed the speaker button and stared into Veronica's eyes as she answered. "Hi, Kaia here."

"Hi, Kaia. It's Lila."

Veronica's eyes grew, becoming big blue disks in seconds. A nerve—fresh, raw, and open—had clearly been exposed in those four words. Kaia reached across the counter and gripped Veronica's hand. Their explosive conversation in the restaurant bathroom flashed through her mind. And now that she understood Veronica better, she knew what was on the line.

Kaia could take the phone off speaker and slip into the bedroom behind the closed door. But that would leave Veronica alone in the kitchen, her mind filled with questions. Instead, Kaia continued to hold Veronica's hand, flashed her a grin, and spoke into the phone. "Hey, Lila.

What's up?"

"Long time no talk."

"Yeah. I've been busy. Sorry about that." Kaia squeezed Veronica's hand in an attempt to inject every molecule of affection she felt in that small action.

"Me, too. But I'm free this weekend, and I wondered if you wanted to get together."

"Actually, since we last talked, I started dating someone." Kaia penetrated Veronica with her gaze and got a sweet smile in response.

"Oh…well…that's okay. I'm not necessarily looking for something exclusive."

Kaia's head jerked back. She hadn't expected that response. Her impression of Lila had been just the opposite. Presented with this response, Kaia had no choice but to make a hard move.

Kaia had never been as sure about someone in so short a time as she was about Veronica in that moment. Being forced into a corner shouldn't feel so right.

Kaia spoke clearly into the phone. "Yeah. Well, it's serious with this one."

That simple statement charged the air in the little kitchen. What Lila said after that was white noise. Kaia managed to answer politely and hang up before she caught Veronica in her arms as she leaped over the island and pressed their lips together.

****

Veronica's office felt like a stifling box compared to Kaia's cozy kitchen filled with love and kisses. It didn't matter that the room was covered in edgy modern art. The fact that her private space alone was twice the size of Kaia's little cooking nook seemed irrelevant. And the massive wooden desk and cushy leather chair could never compete with the hard barstool and chipping linoleum of Kaia's island.

But Monday morning brought responsibilities that

couldn't be ignored. With three active murder cases and nearly a dozen other wrongfully accused women she needed to defend against drug charges, robbery, and in one case, child abuse for a small boy with a rare disease, there was no time for lazing about with the woman of her dreams.

She'd reluctantly dragged herself away from Kaia's perfect figure and into her twelfth story office in the financial district. There was too much work to do to stay in that warm bed wrapped around the soft body of the person she'd easily fallen in love with.

Veronica shook her head in a vain attempt to clear it of all things Kaia, and tried to refocus on the email she'd just received from a private investigator she hired to look into Gregory's short and seedy life.

She was still re-reading the paragraph that detailed his complex relationship with a distant cousin, who appeared to have once worked for the SFPD, when she was snapped out of her concentration by Mia's voice on the speaker box of her phone. "Call from Detective Poll for you. Do you want to take it?"

Veronica slammed her finger on the button that allowed her to talk back. "Yes. Of course."

Before Mia could answer, she picked up the receiver. "Detective?"

He wasn't on the line yet, still caught up in the transfer between Mia's line and her own private one in the office. Frustrated, she spoke again when a slight sound change indicated he could hear her. "Detective Poll?"

"Hello, Ms. Turner. How are you?"

Ugh. Small talk. Did they really have to do this right now with so much on the line? "I'm fine. What's going on?"

"I'm calling to let you know that a search warrant has been executed on the residence of Linda Rosen. Prosecutor McAdams wanted you to know."

Breath escaped her lungs as if it had been held captive for years. "Okay. That's good news. When will you know more?"

"I'll keep you apprised of everything as I'm able. Obviously, we're hopeful the search will turn up something valuable in the case of Gregory French's disappearance.

"What about Giles?"

"At this time I don't have any information about his involvement in the Gregory French case. But based on his connection to Linda Rosen and yourself, I've asked him to come in for an interview."

"And?"

A creepy static filled the line and drew out each second until Poll finally answered. "He's thinking about it."

Which meant—hell no. Veronica's fingers ran along the hem of her skirt in a nearly involuntary fiddle. She couldn't completely articulate what it was about Giles that had her so on edge. It was as if the information that might provide insight was locked up in her brain, unable to help her. Frustration didn't even begin to cover it.

"I understand that Gregory is related to an ex-cop. Did you know that?"

"I did. I've already interviewed former Officer Briggs."

"And?"

"I can't tell you about that. But I have talked to him. He doesn't seem to be involved."

"He doesn't seem to be involved, except what?"

"Outside of discussing police techniques with Gregory, Briggs appears to be completely clear of any involvement in anything I'm investigating."

Veronica could read between the lines. She understood that Poll was telling her Gregory had asked his cousin a bunch of sketchy questions. With nowhere else to go, she ended the conversation. "Thank you for the call, Detective. And for keeping me apprised of the situation. I look forward to hearing from you again soon."

She stayed on the line long enough for Poll to say some parting thing before she slammed down the receiver. Veronica sat straight in her chair and stared at the landscape painting on the opposite wall. Despite the good news from Poll, something was still deeply wrong, not just with this case, but with her own involvement in it. She just couldn't put her finger on what it was.

She turned back to the email from the PI. Once she'd finished combing through it and taking thorough notes, she went back to the notes she'd taken about Gregory, trying to piece together the puzzle of who he was, what he'd done, and most important, why he disappeared.

There were several connections to be made. But she needed to visualize it. Veronica grabbed her laptop and took it to a small credenza in the far corner of her office. In the space between the window and short wall of the room Mia had installed a large whiteboard. She insisted that would be a much better workspace for Veronica than the multiple pieces of scrap paper taped together into a wonky makeshift map Veronica had used for years.

She grabbed the worn eraser and did her best to clear up the past words and lines that still echoed through the glossy white surface in tones of blue, green, and red. She dropped the eraser on the small shelf installed at the base of the board and grabbed her favorite marker—the blue one—to write Gregory French in the center of the board.

Referring to her notes, she began to create a circle of names around his. She wrote down Linda Rosen, Officer Briggs, Jessica, all their mutual friends, and of course, Giles. From Giles she drew another line that led to her own name, then connected her name with a separate line to Jessica.

By the time she was finished, a web of relationships played themselves out on the board, with lines that bobbed and weaved between all the people. Every line led back to Gregory. Each one another clue.

How long she stared at that abstract art of crime and mystery with the cap of the blue marker pressed against her chin, she wasn't sure. But her whirling mind was redirected by the phone again. Only this time, the call didn't come through Mia.

She threw the marker down on the shelf and marched across the room. There were only a few possibilities of who could be on the other end of the line when a call bypassed Mia. The most frequent was a family member. The second was the jail. And the third would be Kaia.

Hoping for Kaia, Veronica slumped when she realized the call was from the jail. She accepted it and Jessica came on the line. Veronica was on edge the moment she heard the tension in Jessica's voice.

"You have to come here. Now." Completely out of character, Jessica's tone was bathed in pure panic.

"Calm down and tell me what's going on."

"I can't. Not on the phone. Please, come now. It's an emergency."

Chapter Seventeen

The niggling thought that she needed to invest in a good office chair managed to break into the front of her mind briefly as Kaia shifted on the hard kitchen stool. But the small and persistent pain in her lower back wasn't enough to get her to move away from the spot, as she hunched over her tablet.

She scrolled up to read further into Emma's report. Despite Jessica's rant the night before about what a waste of money it was for she and Agnes to invest in a PI for the podcast when she had several on her payroll, Kaia was grateful for Emma.

Emma worked independently for *Murder by the Bay*. This kept her from being tied down by any loyalty to Veronica or her clients. With the lines clearly drawn, Emma felt no pressure for the information to lead in any one direction. Instead, she could follow the clues with as much objectivity as possible.

Emma was also a complete detail freak. Kaia shared this characteristic with her, and practically salivated over the long, in-depth reports she received from Emma twice a week. Today's report was an exhaustive review of Jessica's trust. Emma had picked it apart and pointed out details Kaia hadn't seen as important before. But through Emma's eye, they were elevated to a new status.

As Kaia knew, Jessica's trust set aside a fund for her niece. Additionally, the niece couldn't access the funds until she turned 21. The age requirement was set as an additional safeguard to keep Jessica's evil sister-in-law from getting any of the money.

So now that Jessica was locked up, so was the money. Only the trustee had control of it now, and they were only authorized to use it as needed for the care of Pookie. While none of this was hot news to Kaia, Emma had uncovered a tidbit of information Kaia had been unable to find. Like an archaeologist, she brushed away at the dirt with a paint brush until she hit the jackpot of all finds.

It was at the bottom of the report that Kaia saw a notation with the name, address, and phone number of the attorney's office that controlled the funds. At the bottom of the notation was the name of the attorney who served as the trustee.

Giles Mills.

Kaia fumbled on the counter with her left hand, eyes still locked on that name. She managed to get her fingers around her cell phone and bring it to her. She ripped her gaze from the tablet long enough to pull up a contact on her phone and hit send.

"Hey, favorite niece. How are you?"

It was usually a sweet experience to talk with her Uncle Peter. Kaia liked to set aside at least an hour to enjoy their meandering conversations about family and life. But not now. Not today.

"I have a question for you, Uncle Pete. A legal one."

"Aw, kid. You know I'm always happy to help, but I'm just a boring old IRS lawyer. I don't know about the murder and intrigue you deal with on that podcast of yours. It's great, by the way. Your aunt and I are completely sucked in."

"Thanks. So, my question is actually about money."

Uncle Pete's deep chuckle provided a sense of comfort that seemed out of place in the middle of Kaia's intensity. "Okay. Shoot."

"Okay. Let's say a person has their money going into a trust. Could someone else, like say a surviving spouse, get their hands on it?"

Peter didn't even pause. "No."

"There's no way?"

"I mean, unless…"

"Unless what?" Kaia had never been so impatient with her big, sweet uncle before, but she was practically bouncing off the walls now.

"Well, is the spouse also the trustee?"

"No. It's a third party."

"Well, so, technically no. When a person dies, in the case of most trusts, no changes can be made. However..."

"However, what?" Kaia asked.

Peter chuckled. "Well, in my experience trustees aren't always as ethical as they're supposed to be. I've been involved in prosecuting a few."

"What does that mean, exactly?"

"It means they're in charge, and if they determine something is in the intent of the donor, they can do it. Sometimes they like to stretch those definitions. They don't always get away with it legally. But, a criminal trustee, they could do a lot of sneaky things, and if they knew what they were doing, they might just get away with it."

Kaia ran her fingers through her hair, tugging lightly at the ends. "Okay. So. One person is in charge of all that money."

"Yep. That's usually how it's set up. And I've seen some stuff, kid. This one guy, he was in charge of his aunt's money, and he blew it all on trips to Hawaii with his boyfriend. He's on the hook for every dime now."

"So, a crooked trustee might spend the money on themselves?"

"Oh, yeah. Hopefully they'll get caught if they do. But, you know, there's always those that take the money and run to Switzerland." Peter laughed, the sound rich and sweet.

Despite that evocative statement, Kaia managed to get through twenty minutes of what normally would have been a great talk with her uncle. She dutifully asked about her aunt and their beloved Great Dane. By the time she hung up, her mind reeled. Something was wrong with all of this—Gregory, Linda, Giles.

The pieces began to drop into place, and the picture wasn't pretty.

****

Traffic was particularly gnarly. Despite it being nearly ten in the morning, the San Francisco streets were packed with rideshares, taxis, and buses. Not helpful when she was trying to reach Jessica, who appeared to be having a panic attack at the jail.

Veronica glanced in her rearview mirror again. Since leaving the parking garage back at her office, the same red SUV had been tailgating her. Normally, she'd just shoot the driver the finger and go on about her day, but not today.

The tension riding her made every color brighter, every sound louder, and every irritation greater. The man in the red SUV, with his stupid dark sunglasses and out of place baseball cap that announced his fandom for a Giants rival, was nothing short of a major asshole barging into her already stressful day.

She focused on the road in front of her again as traffic began to move. The congestion was so bad she barely cleared the intersection before the light changed again. Without looking, she was certain she must have lost the idiot in the red SUV.

Ready to move toward the jail and her panicked client, Veronica finally took hold of her knowledge of the city streets and turned down an alley she knew would be free of delivery trucks this time of day.

Zooming through the little shortcut appeared to be an easy task as the narrow, brick-lined alley presented a completely clear path to the next major road. But all that changed when her bumper was smacked hard from behind and her head slammed into the seat back.

In a moment of pure instinct, she slammed on the brakes. She pulled her head up despite an aching protest in her neck and put the car in park. Eyes blinking against a blur, she pulled the car door handle and kicked the door open.

It took a moment to hoist herself up, hand pressed against the top of the car to steady her wobbly legs. She twisted around to look at the offending vehicle that had rammed into her.

She'd barely registered that the car pressed up against her bumper was the same red SUV that had been following her when a hand wrapped around her mouth. Her entire body was hoisted up by strong arms.

Despite her legs kicking wildly in the air, she was shoved into the back of the SUV. Her face planted in the vinyl seat as her hands were wrenched behind her and tied with something rough and scratchy.

The screams she pressed into the fabric beneath her mouth were muffled further. She was yanked up by her arms, sending a shooting pain through her shoulders, and a piece of grey tape was slapped over her lips.

She was pressed back onto her stomach, her feet tied together then shoved so her heels hit her ass as the door slammed shut, nearly breaking her kneecaps. The vehicle moved backward then careered wildly before going forward again.

Chapter Eighteen

Kaia and Agnes had once had a really great conversation with a retired detective. They'd been interviewing her for the podcast. She'd told them that even though they were always looking for motive, it wasn't as important in a court of law. Technically, prosecutors don't have to explain motive to a jury in order to convict someone of murder.

So Kaia knew that despite the fact that investigators, reporters, and onlookers always wanted to know why someone committed a crime, knowing it didn't necessarily help get convictions, search warrants, or arrests.

Still, Kaia decided to call Detective Poll. Whatever else there was, Giles Mills had bucket loads of motive, a couple billion of them. Detective Poll had given his card to Veronica, who'd left it pinned to Kaia's refrigerator door with a magnet that featured a sea lion and the logo for the Marine Mammal Center.

Instead of a call operator, Kaia got voicemail. Detective Poll explained on the recording that the caller had reached his cell phone, but he was unavailable at the moment. He promised to call back as soon as he could. Kaia didn't bother to leave a message. Instead, she hung up and immediately called Veronica's cell phone. The phone rang until it too went to voicemail.

Kaia paced in her kitchen from one end of the little island to the next, then swung around and did it again. She bit at her thumbnail and tried to process all the information she had.

Giles Mills definitely had a reason to kill Gregory and frame Jessica—several billion of them. He also had the means. And as the ex-husband of the woman Gregory was having an affair with, he had the means to do both things. Add to that how fishy it was that he had threatened Veronica when she'd gotten too close, and the formula looked clear.

Kaia stalled in her pacing as panic welled up inside her chest. What did that mean for Veronica? If she'd gotten too close to the truth about a man who had committed murder and successfully framed an innocent person, how much danger was she in?

She immediately called Veronica's office. The phone went to voicemail again. Barely able to contain her stress, she called the number that would get her to Veronica's assistant.

"Veronica Turner, attorney at law," Mia answered.

"It's Kaia. Where's Veronica?"

"She left about twenty minutes ago. She said she was headed to the jail to see Ms. French."

"Why? Did she say why? She doesn't have a scheduled meeting."

"No. She didn't say much. She just ran out in a hurry. Told me to reschedule everything."

"Okay. Thanks. Will you call me if you hear from her?"

Kaia didn't register whatever Mia said next. She just turned off the call and called Agnes while moving toward the front door. She gathered her wallet and keys on the way.

"Kaia, what's up?"

"I think Giles Mills is the killer."

"What? Are you sure?"

"Pretty sure. Listen, I can't get ahold of Detective Poll or Veronica. I'm freaking out. I think Veronica went to the jail to talk to Jessica."

"Okay. What can I do?"

Kaia yanked open the door to her apartment. "Can you track down Poll?"

"Sure. What are you going to do?"

Kaia pulled her door closed and locked it. "I'm going to find my girlfriend."

****

Kaia squared her shoulders and stared straight ahead; the most confident, fierce look she could muster plastered on her face. "I need to see Jessica French right away."

She knew that the jail absolutely did not grant unscheduled visits that weren't from detectives or attorneys. That was not something Kaia would let stand in her way, not now, not today.

The officer behind the desk glanced up, her bright blue eyes peered back at Kaia from behind a pair of round wire-framed glasses. It was the same face Kaia had seen during each of her previous visits.

The officer smiled. "Of course." She typed something up on her computer before gesturing toward the signing device on the counter between her and Kaia.

Kaia was almost too shocked to register what happened. When she glanced at the small screen it indicated her name, the time, and under reason the words "on behalf of prisoner's attorney."

Kaia realized in that moment that having been seen with Veronica each time she'd come here had caused the officer to believe she worked for her. Not wanting to dismiss this gift she swiftly signed her name.

Kaia's heart pounded as she followed another corrections officer down a wide hallway. Was Veronica already here? Could she be around the corner, unable to answer her phone? Perfectly safe?

When she saw Jessica already seated on the other side of a Plexiglas shield—the seat opposite her empty—a hollow ache hit her chest. Kaia picked up the receiver on her side of the wall even as she lowered herself into the cold, hard, plastic chair. "Jessica. What's going on?"

"Where's Veronica?" Jessica asked, eyes wide.

"I don't know. I thought she was here. But when I got here I didn't see her car and then—"

"No. She didn't show up. I called her half an hour ago. She promised she was coming. Where is she?" Jessica's voice, high and tight, was infused with sheer terror.

"I don't know. I came here because Mia said she was on her way here."

"She was supposed to come right away. Where is she?"

A clamp of fear pressed on Kaia's chest making speech nearly impossible. But she powered through. Only information could help now. She needed more of it. "Back up. Why did you ask her to come here?"

Jessica closed her eyes and took a deep breath. When her eyes opened again, she spoke, slower and calmer. "I have a regular call with Malcolm every week to talk about how Pookie is doing. He goes and checks on her at Agnes and Helen's and reports back. Anyway, I talked to him this morning. He said he got a weird phone call just before mine. He was about to call Veronica, but my call rang through before he could. The caller was looking for Veronica. The caller said he'd heard Veronica was staying with Malcolm. And Malcolm swore it sounded like Gregory."

Confusion swamped Kaia. "Wait. What? How?"

Jessica took another deep breath. "I thought he had to be mistaken. But here's the thing: Gregory used to pick Pookie up at Malcolm's every now and again if I was busy. Malcolm would know his voice. I called Veronica the minute I got off the phone with Malcolm. I think Gregory is looking for her."

"Wait." Kaia held her hand up, hitting the Plexiglas between them, her palm slapping against it with a pain Kaia almost welcomed. "So, you're saying you think Gregory is alive? And after Veronica?"

"That's exactly what I'm saying."

****

For a dead man, Gregory French was an excellent driver. He managed to get out of the San Francisco congestion and onto the freeway before Veronica even managed to get herself upright in the back seat.

By the time she'd swung her bound feet around, pulled her torso up and scooted in the seat so her arms weren't horribly mangled in the process, she was sweaty and pissed off.

Despite the fear that overtook her body, creating an uncontrollable shaking that vibrated through her entire being, anger was a far more familiar emotion for her, so she clung to it as she watched his stupid face in profile. Every few minutes his beady little eyes hit the rearview mirror and she could attempt to kill him with her gaze.

This usually made him smile or laugh, the bastard. He kept driving, taking them out to the Central Valley where long stretches of highway were framed with nothing but fields of almonds, avocados, and grapes for miles in any direction.

The strain in her shoulders because of the way her hands were tied behind her back created a long-term ache she'd come to mostly ignore, except when the car hit a bump in the road. The chafing on her wrists from the rope was a constant irritant, as was the way her ankle bones were pressed together by the tightly fastened binding on her legs. But the worst of it was the tape over her mouth. It wasn't just physically irritating, it was a personal insult, a symbolic silencing she simply couldn't handle.

"Bet you're surprised I'm alive," Gregory said.

Veronica's only response was a loud, muffled noise emanating from her throat, one that expressed her rising anger as much as possible.

"Or maybe you're not. Maybe you already figured it out. Either way, I needed collateral. May as well take you. After all, with you gone, Jessica doesn't stand a chance." Gregory's cackling laugh made her blood boil.

He quit talking after that, content to drive south in silence, only breaking it when his phone rang. The tone was different from her own phone, which rang just minutes after the kidnapping. He managed to extract it from her jacket pocket even as he drove through the city streets. Once they reached the highway, he chucked it out the window. It was a smart move. It kept her from being tracked by anyone who might be looking for her.

But he did answer his own phone. "Yo. What's up?"

The voice coming from the phone's speaker echoed through the car. "Why the fuck did you come back here?"

"To get my money, dumbass."

"I told you Linda would bring it to you. Now the fucking cops are everywhere." It was this last sentence that brought recognition for Veronica. The voice echoing through the phone, low and sinister, was the same one that had threatened her a few weeks before.

"Giles, I don't trust your ass as far as I can throw you, man. Why did it take so long for me to get my money?" Gregory said.

"Your life is in my hands, asshole. So you better start trusting me. And I told you, this shit is complicated. But you got your money now. Please tell me you're on your way back to Mexico."

"Linda only had like two hundred and fifty grand. You promised way more than that."

Giles let out a heavy sigh. "And you'll get it. But this is what I could get in cash for now. Again, please tell me you're headed to the border, you fucking idiot."

"I am. And I have insurance in the car with me."

"What the fuck does that—" Giles sucked in a breath. "You fucking idiot. What did you do?"

"I took that pain-in-the-ass lawyer that figured everything out. Bitch is in the backseat with a big old piece of duct tape over her mouth. Say hi, honey."

Veronica screamed, the sound far more muted than she desired.

"Jesus Christ. How far are you from the border? Shit is going down here in town. Linda's house got tossed."

"I know. I pulled out as the cops pulled in. Is she okay?"

"She's at a fucking police station right now, what do you think?"

Gregory slammed his fist on the car's center console so hard it sent a deep vibration through the car that blasted into Veronica with a chilling force. "You're a lawyer. Go help her."

"I'm on my way now. Listen, you need to make sure you don't get caught. Under any circumstances. Do you hear me?"

"It's all good man. I won't get caught."

"What about Turner? What are you going to do with her?"

"I'll get rid of her just before I cross the border. In the desert. She won't be a problem ever again."

"Well do it right. Because she told the fucking cops I

threatened her. I don't want any of this shit coming back to me. Do you hear me, asshole?"

"Yeah. Yeah. Don't worry. No one will ever find her."

As the phone went dead and the car was packed with a deep silence again, Veronica knew for certain that this road trip would be a dead end for her.

****

Kaia gripped the phone in her hand, sweat causing the plastic handle to slip down her palm. Her fingers took up the cause, pressing with extreme intensity to keep this one line of information open. "Tell me everything."

Jessica pulled on a lock of hair. "I don't actually know anything."

"You know Gregory," Kaia said. "If he's alive and he has Veronica, why? What? Where? Tell me."

"I can only assume he faked his death to frame me, and get me into jail."

"Why?" Kaia's tone reflected the pain shooting through her chest. "Why Jessica?"

"Money of course." Jessica's bright blue eyes leaked a bit, the tear slipping down her cheek, betraying a heart she usually refused to acknowledge.

"Jessica," Kaia patted her hand against the counter frantically. "Explain it to me! Please."

Jessica sucked in a breath. "Okay. I think he faked his death and made a deal with the guy who holds my trust, Giles. I think this whole thing is about robbing me. And for some reason, Gregory knew or thought that Veronica was on to him. So he kidnapped her on her way here. That's all I can guess. I'm trapped in here." She slammed her hand against the Plexiglas in frustration. "And I can't do a damn thing about it."

Compelled to move, Kaia stood, her torso bent over to accommodate the phone. "Where would he go, Jessica?"

"Mexico. He loves it there. We go a few times a year. He speaks Spanish pretty well. He knows some guys at the border, too. He can come and go as he pleases if he times it right, with whatever he wants in the trunk. You know what I mean?"

Kaia's heart thumped in her chest. Her legs itched to begin a run to her car. "Yeah. I understand. How does he get there?"

"What? Oh, he goes through the valley. Says it's the most efficient. Then drops down at San Diego. That's where his buddy works."

"Thanks." Kaia dropped the phone receiver. She ran toward the jail's exit, only the clanging of the swinging phone hitting the Plexiglas left in her wake.

****

"Kaia, you there?" Agnes sounded nearly as stressed as Kaia felt.

"Yeah, I'm here. What's the word?"

"Ms. Kent. Where are you?" The deep male voice traveled through Agnes's phone unexpectedly.

"Detective Poll?"

"Yeah, Kaia. I'm in his office, along with Malcolm. And we just talked to Jessica."

"Ms. Kent. Where are you right now?" Poll's voice overtook Agnes's quick, rambling speech.

"On the I-5." Kaia didn't take her eyes off the road as she zoomed down the HOV lane, not caring one bit that she didn't qualify to use the carpool lane.

"Why?" A new voice entered the conversation and Kaia could only surmise that it was Malcolm.

"Because Jessica says that's Gregory's preferred route. And my phone agrees. It's the fastest way to Mexico."

"What, exactly, are you attempting to do, Ms. Kent?"

"I'm trying to find my girlfriend, Detective. Too bad you aren't doing the same."

"They are, Kaia. There are CHP officers on it now," Agnes said.

"We agree that I-5 is the best bet," Poll said. "But I've

deployed officers on multiple routes. We've got a description of the car, it's a red SUV registered to Linda Rosen. Red, license plate 5TWH7."

Kaia's mouth opened and closed over and over as if the hinge were busted. "How do you know all this?"

A loud sigh hit the phone sounding like an exasperated wind pushing on the door, wanting to be let in. "We found Ms. Turner's car in an alley. There were witnesses who saw the red SUV ram into her then abduct her. They called it in. We put the pieces together. We're on his trail now."

Kaia glared at the asphalt ahead of her. "And how far behind are we?"

"Not sure. We're still trying to figure that out. But there was an accident on I-5 near Lost Hills. A camera nearby shows he got caught in it. It buys us time. We'll find him."

"Unless I do first," Kaia said.

"Well, Ms. Kent. I was hoping I could talk you into turning around and coming back to the city. I'd like to talk with you while everything is fresh."

"Yes, well, I'd like to get to Veronica before she dies."

"Ms. Kent. Your help will be much more valuable—"

Whatever Detective Poll said next was lost as Kaia hit the button on the phone and the pedal on the truck.

****

The report on the radio sent chills through Kaia. But at least it was something. A nugget of information. The public was to keep their eyes peeled for Gregory French, who was indeed alive, armed, and dangerous. He'd been spotted by numerous witnesses along I-5 now, and was on the run.

Kaia was doing exactly that, keeping her eyes out, as she drove along the highway in search of the red SUV. She planned to confront Gregory, dangerous or not. The ringing of her phone pierced through the sound of the radio. She slammed it and hit the speaker button on her phone.

Agnes's voice echoed through the speaker. "Detective Poll asked me to please get you to come back to the station."

Kaia huffed out her frustration. "Like I said, he can ask me all the questions he wants after I find Veronica."

"Kaia, Poll says Gregory is dangerous. I'm scared for you."

Kaia kept her eyes on the highway in front of her but tilted her head so she spoke clearly into the phone's speaker. "And I'm scared for Veronica. What would you do if it was Helen?"

Agnes sighed. "I get it."

"Of course you do."

"Well, Poll gave me an update."

Kaia gripped the steering wheel. "I'm all ears."

"Linda spilled the goods. Poll's been interrogating her while Malcolm and I have been sitting here. He just came in and confirmed that Linda gave Gregory some money. That's why he came back from Mexico, for cash. She claims she didn't know anything about his plans to kidnap Veronica. He was just supposed to get the cash and take off back across the border."

"Thanks, Agnes. Anything else? Did he say if there were any sightings?"

Agnes's voice was strained and quiet. "Not since the back-up due to the accident."

That was almost forty-five minutes ago now. As much mileage as Kaia may have gained on him, there was no telling if it was enough. A CHP motorcycle flew past her on Kaia's right. Kaia sped to stay on its tail as it bobbed and weaved through traffic.

Kaia was certain of one thing, the officer was looking for Gregory, just like she was. Kaia sent them a good luck wish and continued scanning the cars around her.

"Thanks, Agnes. I gotta go now." Without waiting for niceties, Kaia hung up.

Seconds later an unfamiliar pinging sound had her glance down at her dash. The truck was nearly out of fuel. Kaia realized she'd just passed the last small town and was faced with at least twenty miles of nothing but orchards and farms stretching out ahead of her.

She'd be no good to Veronica at all if she were stuck on the side of the road, baking in the valley heat with no gas.

Chapter Nineteen

Veronica was a firm believer in the electric car—fully ready for the world to leave its dependency on gas—but the need for fossil fuel in this moment had led Gregory to pull into a dusty, isolated station tucked in against the highway in the middle of the central valley.

He'd reached behind him to rip the duct tape off her mouth as he veered off the exit. Other than the small shout that accompanied the sharp pain of the tape attempting to cling to her skin as it was violently pulled away, Veronica stayed quiet. She had nothing to say to Gregory French.

"Listen up. I may have removed that tape, but if you make a fucking sound, I'll pistol whip your ass and you'll wake up next week with a headache like you've never had in your life."

"Then why take it off, asshole?"

Gregory slammed his fist against the steering wheel and sucked a breath through his teeth. "Because, dumbass, I don't want the fuckers in the gas station to see you looking like a fucking kidnap victim."

"Except I am, asshole."

Gregory jolted the car to a stop at the gas pump and twisted in his seat to glare at her. Veronica didn't meet his eyes, instead she stared down at her bound feet. The little piece of twine he'd wrapped around them presented the biggest challenge to getting into that store with the dirty windows perched just twenty feet away from that damn pump.

"Listen. I need you until we get to the border," he said. "Just in case. So I'd rather not pop you right here." Veronica looked up long enough to catch a glimpse of the gun he'd revealed when he flipped down the glove compartment. The flash of black metal momentarily caught her gaze then bounced away again. "But I will if you don't sit there and act like you're a nice passenger lady. Kay? Slap an expression on your face like you're having the best Uber ride of your life. Got it?"

Veronica nodded, eyes still focused on the twine winding around her ankles. Despite how tight it was, it held a major flaw. Gregory hadn't tied it. He'd merely wrapped it around her ankles a few times.

Even as he heaved his body out of the car, she began to shift her feet back and forth, stretching the twine a tiny bit each time. By the time she heard the click of the nozzle hit the gas tank, her ankles were raw and sore but there was nearly enough room to get a foot through the rope.

Seconds later, her feet were free. The rope tying her hands was most definitely fully fastened. She could feel the large knot press against her wrist. She wouldn't have the same luck there. There was nothing to do but yank her left shoulder nearly out of socket so her right hand could pull on the door handle.

She shoved her torso into the door and toppled out onto her back as it gave way. She rocked forward and pushed to her feet just as Gregory shouted out to her. But she didn't stop to look at him. Instead, she bolted forward and careened into the glass door.

With no hands to pull it open, she gave the door a hearty kick and backed up six inches. The distinctive sound of the car door opening reached her ears. Gregory was either planning to flee or get his gun. Veronica didn't have time to contemplate what would happen if he chose the latter.

The glass door swung open and a woman's thin arm catapulted out and yanked Veronica into the stuffy little store. She fell forward, face headed toward the linoleum flooring, but the woman caught her. A young man moved around the store's counter to join them.

"Help me," Veronica whispered.

"We got you, honey. We got you." The woman moved with Veronica deeper into the store, tugging as Veronica's shoes slipped on the slick black and white checkers beneath them.

"Get back there," the young man shouted. He waved one long arm toward the back of the store where a worn wooden door was cracked open. With the other hand he reached toward the front door.

The shape of his hand was clear. Cupped and ready, it reached for the big, steel lock. But he wasn't fast enough. The door swung open. Gregory shoved his way inside, his terrifying black gun pointed right at the kid's nose.

****

The stress of the little gas light on her dashboard was a drop in the bucket compared to that of knowing the woman she loved had been kidnapped and could be anywhere between San Francisco and Mexico. But it was enough to send Kaia emotionally over the edge.

Through the cloud of her tears she spotted the lone gas station sitting beside an otherwise neglected highway exit. She managed to get off in time and make it toward the station. But as she approached, it became clear that something wasn't right.

With no living soul in sight, a still running vehicle sat with the gas being pumped and no human anywhere to babysit it. In fact, the nozzle had fallen out of the gas tank and lay near the vibrating exhaust.

The gas pump's safety mechanism prevented gas from spilling everywhere. As she pulled her truck into a spot along the edge of the lot, away from the pumps, Kaia realized with shock that the abandoned vehicle was the red SUV she'd been searching for, its front bumper dented and coated in the same white paint as Veronica's car.

Kaia threw the truck into park and raced to the SUV. Still and empty, the vehicle stood like a terrifying beacon. The back door hung open, a piece of duct tape lying on the seat.

Kaia slowly raised her head, squinting to see inside the glass door of the gas station. The sun skipped past the windowed door, allowing her the view of a silhouette of a man, his arm raised, gun pointed at some unseen foe.

Against every bit of common sense, Kaia ran back to her truck, wrenched open the passenger-side door, and threw open the glove compartment. A few rustling movements and she extracted a packet of matches. Kaia gripped the small square of cardboard and sulfur and ran back to the red SUV.

****

Scruffy brown hair covered the head and neck pressed up against Veronica's face. Long arms spread out in front of her and the woman beside her. "Just stop right there." The kid's voice cracked and trembled. It was the third time he'd uttered the same phrase since beginning the long journey from the door to the shop to this dead end.

"Get out of my way, kid." There was no fear in Gregory's voice, only menace. He moved closer to the doorway.

The kid tried to step back, but Veronica and her companion were already shoved against the wall of the small closet, their legs jammed between a faded yellow mop bucket and a stack of boxes proclaiming they held the best one-ply toilet paper available. There was nowhere else to go, no way to escape.

Even as the side of a cold blade touched her arm just before the woman beside her cut her bindings, Veronica kept her gaze trained on Gregory. He cocked his hip. For a man holding a gun he looked at ease. He glanced over his shoulder. He stood in the perfect position of power. Ahead of him, cowering in the closet, were his prey. To his right the entire shop sprawled out, and he had a straight-line view of the glass door.

A good four feet separated him from the doorway to the closet Veronica and her would-be rescuers were huddled in. But Gregory clearly wasn't worried about giving them their space. He seemed to realize, as surely as Veronica did, that there was no way for them to escape. Three walls held them together, Gregory's frame in the doorway held them in.

With the confidence of a man who knew he had the upper hand, Gregory smirked. "You can get out of the way, kid, or you can die trying to protect her."

"I'm not moving."

Veronica had to hand it to the kid, he was brave as hell. She patted his bicep. "It's okay. I don't want you to get hurt."

"No. I'm not moving." The kid's voice grew stronger.

"Me neither." The woman beside Veronica nearly pierced her eardrums with her high-pitched declaration.

"There's no point in being a hero here, kid. You don't even know what's up. Maybe I'm a bounty hunter and she's an escaped murderer."

"My name is Brian, not kid. And I don't buy that for a second."

A deep, sinister chuckle erupted from Gregory. "Kid, I drew my own blood for months, arranged my own murder, and been back and forth from Mexico. If you think I'm gonna let a little punk like you stand in my way—" Gregory's head snapped to the side. "What the hell?"

The pulsating sound of sirens echoed through the air outside. It reached the back of their little closet just as Gregory turned his head. Brian lunged forward. Veronica's heart raced as time slowed. Brian's hand moved toward the gun, but before he could get there, Gregory whipped around again and took a step back.

A click echoed through the store and all three captives shivered, their closeness creating a wave effect as it reverberated through their bodies.

Gregory shoved the gun toward them. Brian's body slammed back, causing Veronica's breath to whoosh out of her lungs. "Did you do something?"

"Yeah, jackass. I pushed the panic button." The fear that had been in Brian's voice before morphed to defiance. Veronica wanted to give this kid a freaking medal. No matter how this ended, he and his girlfriend were the best kind of people. If she lived, she'd make sure they never had any kind of legal trouble in their lives.

"Fuck!" For the first time since he'd entered the store Gregory's eyes were wide and alert. He jerked again, shoving the gun forward. "Good thing I have hostages." Gregory smirked. "In fact, I have an even better idea. You can just go out there and tell them you pushed the button by accident. I'll stay here with your girl and the lawyer." He waved the gun to the side, as if commanding Brian to move with its barrel. "You can do that, or they can die."

Brian didn't move. Nor did he address Gregory's threat. "Won't work. Look out there. I bet there's a whole S.W.A.T. team and shit."

Gregory stepped back slowly. One foot creeping behind him, the next feeling its way. He kept his gaze on his captives as he moved out of the doorway and into the main part of the store, gun still firmly pointed at the trio. Veronica's heart pounded in her ears in time with the pulsing sounds outside. Gregory turned his head. His jaw slammed down. Then he spun, pivoting on one heel, and disappeared into the store.

****

The fire wasn't big at all. There must have been too many fail-safes in the gas pump mechanism. But a small puddle of spilled gas did light on the concrete, creating a bit of a show. From her spot near the side of the building, Kaia could see the impression it made. Orange flames licked at the SUV's tires. In the waning light it sent out a halo of red-orange light around the vehicle, making it appear lit up from behind.

Her heart jumped in her throat as the glass door of the shop flung open, jangling the bell suspended above it. A man shot out, tall and lean, tousled brown hair flying around his head, a thick, black gun gripped in his hand.

The man tore at his hair with his free hand and jumped from one foot to the other. But before he could decide what to do about the flames licking around the perimeter of the car, two police cars, sirens roaring, squealed into the gas station lot. The vehicles stopped on a dime and four officers jumped out.

The man with the gun—who absolutely had to be Gregory—spun to head back into the shop. Before her brain could even register what her body was doing, Kaia jumped into action. She ran to the door and plastered her body in front of it.

Kaia squeezed her eyes shut. Throwing herself in the way of a gun-wielding kidnapper was not her brightest move. Unable to watch the coming of her own death, she kept her eyes closed. But every other sense in her body heightened, as if attempting to thwart her plan to stay ignorant of her precarious situation.

The sirens created a backdrop to tense shouting. Beneath the cadence of the voices wafted the clicks and clacks of various gun parts. The smell of burning gasoline, its heat now diminished, lingered, pricking at her nose.

A thud from up ahead hit her ears followed by more clacking sounds, metal on pavement perhaps? A moment later the door at her back vibrated, creating a full body panic. She leapt forward, eyes thrown open.

In front of her, Gregory lay facedown on the greasy, black pavement, a police officer straddling his back. A wispy cloud of grey smoke hung over them like an ominous warning.

Kaia had only a nanosecond to register the scene before the commotion behind her took over her thoughts. The door swung open as she turned toward it, barely escaping a broken nose as she pulled out of the way. A kid, long and lanky, appeared, his hands held above his head as he focused on the police officers.

"Who's inside?" One officer's voice was loud and clear as she shouted toward the kid.

"My girlfriend, Gwen, and the lady he kidnapped." The kid pointed with the toe of his running shoe at the man on the ground.

Kaia's heart nearly stopped. Her head swiveled toward the door. It swung closed with a definitive thump. Her angle had changed, and now the dust-smeared glass obscured the view of anything or anyone that may lie beyond it.

"Anybody hurt?" the officer asked.

The kid kept his hands over his head, even though the police lowered their weapons. He glanced down at the man on the ground. "He had a gun. He pointed it at us."

Why didn't the kid answer the question? Was anybody hurt?

"We got the gun," an officer replied.

"He ran out when he saw the flames. Weird, huh?" The kid stared at the assailant. "One minute his only concern was getting the woman away from me and my girlfriend. Then he thought his car was in danger and he just took off. People's priorities."

"Kid, is anybody hurt?" one of the police officers asked again.

The kid shook his head. At the same moment the door swung open again. A skinny young woman emerged with her arms wrapped around a disheveled blonde that Kaia would know anywhere.

Veronica's gaze was pointed squarely on Gregory's prone body. It was clear she didn't see Kaia until Kaia snagged her waist with one hand and yanked Veronica into her chest. The feel of Veronica, warm and safe in her arms took over every molecule of Kaia's being, every thought, every breath.

"Please tell me you're okay," Kaia pleaded.

"I'm okay. I'm okay. What the hell are you doing here?" Veronica moved back and framed Kaia's face with her hands. Tears streamed down her cheeks.

"I was looking for you. And I ran out of gas."

Veronica sniffed. "Really? You ran out of gas?"

Kaia nodded, a tear of her own spilling onto Veronica's fingers.

Hands pulled them apart gently and moved them to the far end of the parking lot. A fire engine arrived. Unimpressed with the tiny circle of flame Kaia had created, they focused on their four victims, checking everyone over for bumps and bruises.

Gregory was shoved into the back of a police car. The gun was put in a baggie. Someone ran yellow tape across the gas station door.

Kaia, Veronica, Brian and Gwen sat on the grass beneath a bright yellow streetlamp and waited to speak with Detective Poll, who was apparently on his way. They sat in two clumps. Veronica tucked into Kaia's lap, mirroring the way Gwen was tucked in Brian's.

"How old are you anyway?" Veronica asked the two

brave kids.

"I'm nineteen. I'll be twenty in two months. Gwen just turned twenty." Brian flashed a big, toothy grin.

"You're awfully young for superheroes," Kaia said. "But that's exactly what you are. You saved Veronica's life." She squeezed her arm around Veronica's waist as if to emphasize how grateful she was for everything she had in her arms.

Brian blushed, the reddish tinge to his cheeks clashing with the sickly yellow light overhead. "Nah. We just did what anyone would do."

"Yeah," Gwen said. "We don't like bullies. Bullies can fuck off. And that dude—"

"Was dangerous," Veronica said, the shaking in her voice not quite completely gone yet.

"Yeah, well. We all lived," Brian said.

"But we might not have," Veronica said.

This seemed to really resonate with Brian. He stared down at Gwen as if he'd suddenly found his fear of death. "Damn. Yeah. I guess so, huh."

"How can I ever repay you?" Veronica asked. "Lifetime legal services?"

Brian ripped his gaze away from Gwen to look at her. "Hopefully we won't ever need them."

"I know," Gwen said. "You know the *True Crime Tonight* people right? Cause you do the podcast and stuff?

A little flustered by the fact that total strangers out in the valley knew her by name, Kaia merely nodded.

"I am dying to meet Heath."

"Heath?" Brain asked.

"The co-anchor. He is a-maz-ing."

Despite Brian's look of trepidation, Kaia couldn't resist the love-struck expression on Gwen's face or the urge to give her anything she wanted in life. Since seeing that young girl cradle Veronica in her arms as they left the store, she'd become an icon for Kaia.

"I know Heath very well. And I'll make sure that happens for you. I promise."

Gwen's answering scream pierced the evening sky.

"What the hell? Is someone hurt over here?" Detective

Poll's gruff voice accompanied his figure ambling toward them. He looked older than the last time Kaia had met him face-to-face. But she understood how the frantic drive through the valley could do that to a person. She felt at least ten years older herself. Only the feel of Veronica in her arms could battle the lingering stress.

"Believe it or not, happy, Detective." Veronica moved to stand, but Poll reached out his hand to stop her.

He dropped, rather unceremoniously, into an awkward sitting position on the grass facing both couples. "Is that right? Happy to be alive I imagine."

"Among other things," Kaia said.

Poll reached across the thick, green grass to present his hand to Gwen and Brian. "Detective Poll. I hear you two saved the life of the most feared attorney this side of the Sierra Nevadas."

"Is that all I get? The Sierra's?" Veronica asked.

Poll chuckled, the sound soothing. None of them was behaving as if they'd just been through a great trauma, and that was alright by Kaia. Not only did she truly believe that there was no "one way" to behave after a life-or-death situation, but she also believed in meeting victims on their own terms. Obviously, the venerable Detective Poll felt the same way.

"Listen, I know it's been a long night. So we're just going to do a quick rundown of what happened. Then I'm going to ask all of you to come into the station tomorrow and we'll do the long version, okay?"

Gwen and Brian nodded cautiously.

"And we're taking you two back to the city with us. We'll put you up in a hotel tonight. That all right?"

The unsure acquiescence quickly became big grins as Brian and Gwen easily accepted the offer.

"Not a city-paid hotel," Veronica said. "No way. Put 'em in the Radisson. I'll pay."

"Done." Poll grinned, made a notation in his notebook, then slammed it shut. He looked up at the four people sitting opposite him on that little square of grass outside a broken down old service station under a set of blinking street lamps. "Listen, I know this is going to be a hard road for all of you. What happened here today is not the end. It's the beginning. There will be long days of statements, additional visits, depositions, and eventually testimony in court. It's a lot."

The somber mood Poll had cast on the little gathering penetrated Kaia's heart. She stroked the back of Veronica's hand. This reality morphed her relief into a new kind of stress.

"But he won't get away with it will he?" Brian asked.

"Not if I have anything to say about it." Poll had no sooner uttered those words than his phone emitted a cacophonous ring. "Damn." With a groan that would have given the loudest creaky door competition in a spooky movie, he stood. "I need to take this. I'll be right back. Just a little bit longer. Kay?

Kaia watched as Poll left their oasis under the light and disappeared into the crime scene. Despite his absence, his words lingered.

"Gwen. We need to act, now." Brian's sudden enthusiasm seemed completely out of place.

"What? What are you talking about?" Gwen asked.

"Brian, are you alright?" Veronica spoke on the heels of Gwen's question.

"Yes. I am. I just realized how fucked up life is. And I'm going to grab it by the horns. Will you marry me?"

Gwen let out another ear-splitting scream that might have been a yes. The crying that followed sealed the deal though. Kaia kept her eyes on Veronica as she watched them kiss through streaking tears and broken professions of love.

She kissed Veronica's cheek gently. "Wanna do something drastic, too?"

Veronica practically whispered her answer. "Like what?"

"Move out of your crappy little place and into mine?"

"You want me to move in with you?"

Kaia pulled Veronica close and whispered in her ear. "Yes, I want to be here with you for every minute of what's to come."

Chapter Twenty

Veronica shook her head. "It's stupid to be this nervous."

Kaia stopped in mid-motion, abandoned the knife in her hand and the apple she was slicing to lean over the kitchen island and grasp Veronica's hand. "Don't say that."

"No, I mean it. First of all, it's been six months since you told me this dog was coming."

Kaia grinned. "And five months since you moved in with me."

"Yeah, and so I've had a lot of time to adjust to the idea. But now it's happening. It's really happening."

A frown painted Kaia's face. "Veronica. You weren't this worked up about testifying in court last week."

"Court is fine. I can do court. Apparently, even as a victim. And with stupid Gregory and crazy Linda both taking plea deals, I got off easy."

Kaia frowned. "But Giles Mills is pleading not guilty. And when we finally get to his trial you'll have to testify."

"Don't worry, Kaia. He's just trying to save his skin. He's already been disbarred and soon he'll get convicted of conspiracy and probably for fraud with Jessica's trust, too. He'll get jail time. Besides, I don't want to talk about any of them. We have a living being coming to our house any min-ute now."

Kaia chuckled and stood up, letting her hand slip out of Veronica's. "Yes. That's true."

"Tell me again what it is? It's not anything like Pookie is it?"

Kaia laughed. "No. Believe me, no one, not even Malcolm would attempt to train Pookie as a service animal. She's a Lagotto Romagnolo."

"One. I cannot say that. Two, no one in the world has ever heard of that dog."

"That's because they are the second rarest breed in the world. They're used for truffle hunting in Italy and they have incredible noses."

"Hence, she can smell gluten."

Kaia grinned. "Yep. She can smell gluten. And Malcolm has been training her to behave in public, so she can go everywhere with us."

"Everywhere. Great."

Veronica had never been a dog person. She'd never been a people person either. She was good at law. That's what she was good at. But now everything was upside down. Kaia was her life now. They talked and communicated and made love. They were a team.

For the first time since her trust had been so deeply broken by Lane, she'd let someone outside her family into her own, private world. She'd opened up her heart and her life to Kaia and invested her whole self in "them."

But now they were about to go from a twosome to a threesome. There would be a ball of fluff with them everywhere they went. The thing would go to the grocery store, restaurants, everywhere. It would be with them all the time.

Just last night Kaia revealed that she didn't intend for the dog to sleep at night on the fluffy—and quite expensive—dog bed that now took up a portion of the living room. No, she thought the dog should sleep with them in the new California King Veronica had insisted they get for the bedroom.

Veronica wasn't sure she was ready to share Kaia with another being. But she could get over that because it was trained to keep Kaia from falling ill. And that overruled her selfish desire to be number one.

But what if Kaia's new best friend—this being that was meant to literally save her life—didn't like Veronica? She hadn't been brave enough to express this concern out loud. It felt stupid. When had she ever cared if anyone liked her? Why should she care if a dog liked her?

"I got a text from Jessica today." Kaia looked up from the bowl she'd placed the apple in. It was halfway to a fruit salad now. She reached for the cantaloupe as she spoke.

"Ugh. Did she ask you out again?"

Kaia laughed. "Maybe. She sounds like she's doing well, though. I'm happy for her."

"She is. She talks to her sister-in-law and niece now, and she's thrown herself into a new project. Not pillows this time, thank God."

"I heard. She's doing a line of dog stuff."

Veronica rolled her eyes. "I suppose once it's out we'll be swimming in it."

Kaia grinned. "Probably."

The silence that followed was broken by a knock at the door. Veronica's stomach churned. This was it.

Kaia bounded over to the door, her step light and bouncy. Veronica trailed behind her, each movement heavy and slow.

Kaia swung open the door. Veronica peered over her shoulder. Malcolm stood there, straight and tall, a wide grin on his face. Beside him, seated regally, was a light brown, fluffy beast with golden eyes and a pink tongue sticking out of a smiling mouth.

"This is Leona," he announced.

Kaia made an unintelligible sound from the back of her throat and clasped her hands beneath her chin like a child seeing a loaded Christmas tree for the first time.

"Leona, go say hi," Malcolm said.

With his command, the dog stood. It wasn't very big, medium-sized at best. Its curly little head hovered around Malcolm's knees. It moved gracefully toward Kaia, who bent over to greet it.

Kaia didn't touch the animal. She let it thoroughly sniff her. Then it nudged her knee with its shiny, wet nose. That's when she put her hands on its face and started to pet and nuzzle it.

"I used your clothes to get her accustomed to your scent," Malcolm said.

Kaia moved back into the apartment and the dog and Malcolm followed her. Veronica kept pace, staying behind Kaia and away from the dog. Once they were all inside, Malcolm closed the door. Kaia planted a kiss on the dog's muzzle and looked back at Veronica.

The expression on her face was sheer joy. Veronica had

given Kaia that look before herself, but now it was a fuzzy beast that planted the smile on Kaia's lips. As jealously rose in her gut, Malcolm said something unexpected. "I also gave her your sweatshirt, Ronnie. The one you left at my place."

Veronica's gaze shot to him, a man she'd once trusted. He'd given a dog her possessions? Why the hell would he do that?

Before she could ask him about his bizarre betrayal, the dog moved away from Kaia and toward her. Veronica instinctively took a step back. But the thing kept coming toward her. Eventually, her legs hit the couch and she had nowhere to go. Worse yet, she'd been moving with greater speed than she realized and ended up folding at the knees and collapsing onto the couch.

This allowed the beast to fully compromise her space. It leapt up easily, settling itself in her lap. Light eyes stared up at her. There was something in those big, golden orbs, something so real, so true.

A long, pink tongue came out and slowly licked her palm, two licks. Then she stopped and looked up again, pleading.

"Leona," Veronica whispered.

A long, brown tail swirled in an erratic circle accompanied by that silly doggie smile. And just like that, Veronica was in love.

About the Author

Benna Bos is an author, non-profit manager, and adjunct professor of Anthropology. Her greatest love is romance. Mixing Cozy Mystery with engaging love stories, Benna plays on her love of place and her obsession with true crime podcasts. San Francisco is the setting she is most obsessed with, and it happens to be her current home. Benna loves to read, write, play with her dog, and go on road trips.

Another Book By Benna Bos

Investigating Helen

Dr. Helen Nims is hauled into the police station when her new girlfriend is found murdered. Terrified and confused, she finds comfort from a stranger. But when that stranger turns out to be a crime reporter, Helen has to decide if she can be trusted or if confiding in the stunning podcaster will pull Helen deeper into suspicion.

Agnes Coates loves reporting on true crime. But it hits a little close to home when her first crush from high school is found dead in a bathtub. A gorgeous surgeon is tangled up in the police dragnet as they search for the killer, and Agnes must navigate her own feelings as she digs into the mystery and seeks out the truth.

With so much to lose, Agnes and Helen will walk the line between kisses and crime.

Bringing Rainbow Stories to Life

Visit us at our website: www.flashpointpublications.com